Praise for N

. . . if yo[illegible] sex, vio[illegible]
[illegible]iens this is [illegible]

SFX

'As always, Asher is unparalleled at creating
this unique and dangerous environment . . .
as exhilarating as his previous books'

Good Book Guide

'Supreme storytelling confidence . . .
a "first-tier" SF writer'

Interzone

'Close to the violence of splatterpunk, and ideas,
jokes and puns splatter his pages'

Guardian

'Neal Asher is becoming a big name in sci-fi. His
stories revel in their violence and imagination, and
his central character of Ian Cormac is, it seems, here
to stay in the collective consciousness of sci-fi
literature . . . Thoroughly enjoyable stuff'

SciFiNow

'One of the best yet . . . destructive high
Space Opera spectacle'

Starburst

'Straightforward action sci-fi. And, boy, is he good
at that . . . I cannot recommend it highly enough'

Praise for Neal Asher's novels

'Yet another storming performance from the prolific Asher of high-octane violence, exotic tech, and terrifying and truly alien aliens'
Daily Mail

'What has six arms, a large beak, looks like a pyramid, has more eyes than you'd expect and talks nonsense? If you don't know the answer to that, then 1) you should and 2) you haven't been reading Neal Asher (see point 1)'
Jon Courtenay Grimwood

'A powerhouse cocktail of lurid violence, evocative world-building and typically grotesque monsters, but it's amazing how much emotion he's also layered into what could have been a simplistic SF potboiler. Asking difficult questions while still delivering plenty of full-tilt adventure and widescreen action, this is top-notch stuff from an author well and truly at the top of his game'
SFX

'Rail-guns rattle off, pulse rifles fire out shots and explosions ring out. This is what Asher does best'
SciFiNow

'*Shadow of the Scorpion* skilfully combines graphic action and sensitive characterization and is Asher's most accomplished novel to date'
Guardian

PRADOR MOON

Neal Asher was born in Billericay, Essex, and divides his time between here and Crete. His other full-length novels include *Gridlinked*, *The Skinner*, *The Line of Polity*, *Cowl*, *Brass Man*, *The Voyage of the Sable Keech*, *Polity Agent*, *Hilldiggers*, *Line War*, *Shadow of the Scorpion*, *Orbus*, *The Technician* and *The Departure*.

By Neal Asher

Cowl
The Technician

The Owner
The Departure

Agent Ian Cormac
Shadow of the Scorpion
Gridlinked
The Line of Polity
Brass Man
Polity Agent
Line War

Spatterjay
The Skinner
The Voyage of the Sable Keech
Orbus

Novels of the Polity
Prador Moon
Hilldiggers

Short story collections
Runcible Tales
The Engineer
The Gabble

Novellas
The Parasite
Mindgames: Fool's Mate

NEAL ASHER

PRADOR MOON

TOR

First published 2006 by Night Shade Books, USA

First published in Great Britain 2007 by Tor

First published in paperback 2011 by Tor
an imprint of Pan Macmillan, a division of Macmillan Publishers Limited
Pan Macmillan, 20 New Wharf Road, London N1 9RR
Basingstoke and Oxford
Associated companies throughout the world
www.panmacmillan.com

ISBN 978-0-330-52846-7

1 3 5 7 9 8 6 4 2

A CIP catalogue record for this book is available from
the British Library.

Printed in the UK by CPI Mackays, Chatham ME5 8TD

PRADOR MOON

1.

O let us be married! too long we have tarried—

Avalon outlink station lay on the border of the Polity, that expanding political dominion ruled by artificial intelligences and, to those who resented unhuman rule, the supreme autocrat: Earth Central. In the entire history of the Polity only one living alien intelligence had been encountered: an enigmatic entity that for no immediately apparent reason, it being neither ophidian or fire-breathing, named itself Dragon, and ever since spent its time baffling researchers with its Delphic pronouncements. Ruins were found, artefacts certainly the product of very advanced technologies, traces of extinct star-faring civilizations, but no other living sentients. Now a live one had been found.

Avalon, once travelling at one-quarter C, now slowed on the borders of what scientists named, after translation and much academic debate, the Prador Second Kingdom. As Jebel Krong understood it, humans and AIs, though having long been in communication with the entities living in that kingdom, were yet to actually see them. Their ships had been encountered, only to speed away. Probes were sent in to survey the Kingdom worlds and many of them destroyed by the Prador—perhaps understandable caution on their part—but those surviving returned data on high-technological societies based on watery worlds, some pictures of strange organic dwellings, cities, seeming as much at home on land as in sea, and large shoreline enclosures holding herds of creatures like giant mudskippers. However, even those probes were destroyed before returning pictures of the Prador themselves.

However, researchers managed to work out some facts from the data returned. The Prador were creatures at home on both land and in the sea. The design of their ships and some nuances of their language indicated they might be exoskeletal, maybe insectile. They had not developed sophisticated AI, so it seemed likely they were highly individualistic, highly capable as individuals, and definitely somewhat paranoid in outlook. They communicated using sound, and the larger components of their sensorium were compatible with those of humans: their main senses probably being sight and hearing, though scanning of their ships' hulls indicated their ability to see might stray into the infrared with some loss at the other end of the spectrum, and analysis of communications revealed hearing straying into the infrasonic. Their language, just by usage, also indicated a sense of smell as a strong characteristic. Polity AIs claimed, with a certainty above ninety per cent, that Prador were carnivores, hence the corruption of the word "predator" resulting in their name.

But such ominous assertions about these creatures aside, they created, without the aid of AI, a space-faring civilization, a workable U-space drive, and by some quirk of their development it seemed their metallurgical science lay some way ahead of the Polity's. They didn't possess runcibles, which by their very nature of being based on a technology completely at odds with the straight-line thinking of evolved creatures, required AI. From this the Ambassador for humanity felt there to be grounds for constructive dialogue. The Ambassador eagerly anticipated facilitating that dialogue for the technical, moral and social advance of both the human and Prador cultures. It was the kind of thing ambassadors said. Jebel remained highly suspicious, but then, as an Earth Central Security monitor, that came with the territory.

"Their shuttle is now coming in to dock," said Urbanus.

Jebel wore a silver, teardrop-shaped augmentation bonded to his skull behind his left ear, and connected into his mind. He auged into the station network and confirmed the status of the approaching vessel. He studied some of the specs available and did not like what he saw, but at least the mother ship still remained at an acceptable distance. He very definitely did not like the look of that thing: a massive two-kilometre-wide golden vessel, oblate and flattened with some armoured turret on top, many extrusions that were possibly sensory arrays but more likely weapons, and a hull that seemed likely to be armoured with an exotic metal only recently created by Polity metallurgists—one resistant to much scanning, but most importantly one with superconducting crystalline layers that slid against each other, making it resistant to massive impacts and most forms of energy weapon. He frowned, then also checked his messages, since more data might be coming through to him from other sources, and felt a sinking sensation upon seeing just how many awaited his attention. He would have to check most of them later, but one he opened immediately.

TWO BOTTLES OF VIRAGO CHAMPAGNE TO COMPLEMENT A GREEN PRAWN CURRY. ONLY ONE FURTHER INGREDIENT REQUIRED: JEBEL KRONG. SEE YOU AT SIX—CIRRELLA.

Jebel realised he was grinning stupidly and quickly wiped the expression. One of the definite plus points of being seconded to the monitor force here was Cirrella. He hoped this meeting would be brief and without mishap, for then the diplomats and the various xeno experts could take over, and Jebel could enjoy a long-awaited break. Cirrella was a good cook and screwed like every occasion might be her last, and Jebel rather suspected he was falling in love with her.

Now glancing around at the gathered dignitaries, Jebel noted the Ambassador chatting with a group of network reporters, then he focused his attention on his companion. Urbanus looked like a Greek god, but one supplied with grey nondescript businesswear rather than shield and spear. His hair was dark and curly, complexion swarthy, eyes piercing blue. Jebel understood that Cybercorp was debating the merits of actually making their Golem androids ugly so the people who bought their indentures would not feel quite so inferior. Studying Urbanus, he understood why. The Golem made him feel uncomfortable, doubly so when he came to understand that beyond being better looking than him, Urbanus possessed a much larger knowledge base than himself, impeccable manners, and ten times the speed of mind, body and strength.

"Then they're happy with Earth-normal atmosphere and gravity?" asked Jebel.

"So it would seem. Their worlds range from three-quarters to two and a half gravities with atmospheres not much at variance from Earth normal, so it should be within their tolerance."

Jebel already knew all that—only talking because of nerves. He peered up at the hovering holocams, then once again scanned around the chamber constructed especially for this occasion. Auging again, he checked the status of the weaponry concealed in the walls, though really he didn't need to do that since the station AI controlled it.

A boom echoed through the chamber, followed by various clonks and ratchetings as the docking gear engaged.

Specifications for the docking apparatus were transmitted many months ago and this equipment built and installed expeditiously. Jebel focused his attention on the double doors hull-side of the chamber. Their design told him something about the imminent visitors that made him rather nervous. The doors were five metres across and three high. Humans never needed doors so large.

Almost casually Urbanus commented, "I note you are wearing your armour."

"I'm cautious by nature," he replied, frowning, slightly embarrassed that his caution increased since meeting Cirrella. He spoke into his comlink. "Okay guys, you know our remit: only if the AI starts shooting do we draw our weapons, and only then in self-defence. Our prime objective then is to get the Ambassador and all these good citizens out of here. Don't do anything stupid meanwhile… just be ready." Jebel hated this. On the one hand you needed to show trust by meeting openly, and in agreeing to meet on this Polity station the Prador had also shown such trust. However, he could not shake the feeling that the Ambassador, and all the others in this chamber, might be sacrificial pawns in some AI game. Human ambassador—Jebel snorted to himself—everyone knew who the real powers in the Polity were.

The doors clonked, a diagonal split opening and the two door-halves revolving into the wall—as per the Prador design. In the air above Jebel, the holocams of the various news agencies jockeyed for the best view, sometimes smacking rivals aside. He checked the positions of his security personnel, then with Urbanus at his side, moved into position behind the Ambassador as that man moved out before the crowd. Only one other accompanied them: a woman called Lindy Glick—the lower half of her face concealed by hardware made to produce Prador speech, linked up to the aug behind her ear—her presence here only as a precaution since the Prador should be carrying translators.

The smell struck Jebel first; damp, briny and slightly putrid like the odour of flotsam cast up by the tide: decaying seaweed and crab carapaces. He almost expected to hear gulls, but instead heard a heavy clattering from the docking tunnel now revealed. A shadow appeared—one with too much movement in it—and then the Prador came.

There were two of them, each walking on far too many long legs—hence the clattering. These extended from carapaces which from the front resembled pears stood upright and flattened. They scalloped around the rim, purple and yellow, the upper turret of each sporting an array of ruby eyes plus two eye-palps raised up like drumsticks, and mandibles grating before a nightmare mouth. To their fore they brandished heavy crab claws—that being the general impression given. These creatures reminded Jebel of fiddler crabs, though ones with carapaces a couple of metres across.

They swarmed through the doors into the chamber and clattered to a halt before the Ambassador, who took a pace or two back at the sight of these creatures. A stunned silence fell. After a moment the Ambassador found his voice.

"I welcome you to—"

More clattering came from the docking tunnel. The two creatures already in the chamber scuttled sideways in opposite directions towards the sides of the chamber. Two more Prador came out, then two more after them. Finally a larger individual came through—darker than the others and with metallic tech attached to its shell around its grinding mouthparts. This monster was the size of an aircar.

"To coin a cliché," Jebel muttered to Urbanus, "I've got a real bad feeling about this."

Jebel noted a louselike creature the size of a shoe clinging where the big Prador's legs joined to its carapace.

Now the Ambassador got up to speed again. "Prador, I welcome you to the Human Polity. It is with great—"

A crunching hissing bubbling interrupted him, then the flat inflexion-less voice of the Prador's translator turned the sound into words. "I am Vortex, first-child of Captain Immanence."

Jebel wondered how the translator went about selecting those names from the data-bank. They seemed rather ominous, especially when applied to monsters that appeared capable of tearing ceramal. What were these creatures thinking right now? Look at all these soft and chewable food items?

Vortex made its thoughts known. "You humans will surrender this station to us."

Jebel stared in fascination as the smaller Prador to Vortex's left unfolded sets of arms from underneath itself—each ending in complex manipulatory hands which held something that Jebel guessed weren't gifts. One item resembled an old Gatling gun, with heavy cables and something like an ammunition belt trailing back from it to a large box attached to the creature's under-carapace. Another item also trailed cables back to that box. Despite its alien manufacture, Jebel recognised a pulse-gun. The other things they held out were not so easily recognisable, but you just knew you'd rather be on the other side of them.

"You are, at present, the target of many weapons concealed in the walls of this chamber," the Ambassador observed. "I don't know what you hope to—"

Vortex surged forwards, its claws snapping out and open, then closing around the Ambassador's waist. Jebel drew his thin-gun and wished for something heavier as he aimed at the looming Prador. There came a whirring roar as of wind blowing hard down a pipe, then suddenly the chamber filled with deafening noise that drowned out the surge of shouting and screaming. He fired on the Prador, the shots from his weapon only blowing small craters in its hard carapace. Something hit him and jerked him through the air. Subliminally he glimpsed torn-apart human bodies flung piled against the back wall and a blur of missiles tracking up that wall hammering a trenchlike dent.

Rail-gun.

He hit the floor. All around him hot metal fragments rained down. Winded, he rolled and tried to come upright. Weapons ports were open all around. He saw one of the smaller Prador get flung back, its armour smashed so it held to the softer inner body like fragments of shell clinging to a crushed mollusc. Its bubbling scream rose and then abruptly cut off as some explosive projectile detonated inside its body, blowing that away and flinging its limbs bouncing in all directions. Something big penetrated the left-hand wall, detonated inside and blew fire from a large crack, shutting down the weapons ports above. Those of the crowd still able to, were exiting through the rear of the chamber. Jebel tried to put his hand down to shove himself up from the floor, but just did not seem to be able to. A second later he noticed that his right arm ended at the elbow, and that he lay in a sticky pool of his own blood. He sagged back.

Two Golem—monitors like himself—were in close to one of the Prador. They'd lost their clothing and most of their syntheflesh so it seemed two shiny skeletons attacked the crablike creature. They were systematically tearing off its limbs. Another of the creatures staggered around in a circle, with the top half of its carapace completely missing and a grotesque stew of exposed organs bubbling inside. Vortex now backed towards the entrance tunnel, still holding the struggling Ambassador, its remaining three comrades covering its retreat. Next came two crumps, and two of the three Prador disappeared, spraying limbs and carapace and boiled pink flesh everywhere. Something like a piece of liver a metre long slopped down over Jebel's legs, bubbling and smelling of cooked prawns.

"Not good. Not good at all." Urbanus was suddenly beside him, tying a piece of wire above his arm stump then hauling him to his feet. Golem hurtled towards Vortex and the remaining smaller Prador. Few humans remained in the chamber—living ones, anyway. Vortex seemed to ponder the situation for a second, then its claw snicked and the Ambassador fell in two halves to the floor. The Prador now held out that bloody claw. A flash of turquoise cut the air—some kind of particle cannon actually concealed in the claw. Three of the Golem were down, their ceramal bones fused or shattered. A missile struck the big Prador's shell and ricocheted into the wall above, exploding there. As the smoke cleared Jebel saw Vortex pushing forwards, firing that cannon again and again into the weapons ports, and from out behind the creature, those smaller Prador surged, some scrambling over each other in their eagerness. As Urbanus dragged him through the crack in the armoured wall, Jebel glimpsed one of the new arrivals picking up a severed human leg and tearing the flesh from the bone with its mandibles, eating it.

Right, thought Jebel, *big hostile aliens with a taste for human flesh.* It was the kind of scenario that would have been laughed out of the door by a modern holofiction producer.

Jebel could not have been less amused.

The aseptic white walls of Aubron Sylac's surgery enclosed gleaming chrome and chainglass, and all the glass seemed to be glittery sharp. Moria guessed that Sylac's assistant—a partial catadapt girl with cropped black hair and a decidedly pneumatic figure crammed into some premillennial nurse's uniform—was there to put at ease those customers whose sexual penchant ran that way. Sylac certainly did not need much in the way of assistance, what with the pedestal-mounted autodoc crouched over the operating slab. Moria eyed the thing, with its forceps, chainglass scalpels, saws, cauterizers and cell-welding heads mounted on many-jointed arms, it looked like the underside spread of an arachnophobic's chrome nightmare. She eyed Sylac, who wore a heavy, grey aug the shape of a broad bean behind his ear on the side of his bald head. The man did not wear surgical whites, he wore a thick apron and seemed to Moria a reincarnation of some ancient horror film star. What was the name? Horis Marko ... no, Boris Karloff. Moria considered turning round and walking out right then. But that would be defeat.

The new cerebral augmentations at first frightened Moria, as did those people who so willingly had them installed, but, when working with runcible technology, you hit a ceramal ceiling unless you were a natural genius or you augmented. Moria hit that ceiling long ago and now, according to many, had been promoted beyond her abilities on the Trajeen gate project. It was hard enough that the only human to truly understand runcible technology was its inventor Iversus Skaidon. He invented the whole science in the brief time his mind survived direct interface with the Craystein AI. Now it was accepted that unaugmented humans stood no hope of fully encompassing it all—only AIs truly did that. But it was doubly difficult to be sidelined into administration by younger technicians who augmented.

"The Netcom 48," said Sylac, holding up that item.

Smaller than Sylac's own, the polished copper aug bore the same bean shape. It was probably better, but aug tech had yet to attain the stage where upgrading became a simple affair. It was not quite like replacing the crystal in your personal computer—brain surgery never was—so Moria understood why Sylac retained the one he wore.

"Yes, that's the one," Moria replied, as she finally stepped over the threshold.

"If you please." Sylac gestured with one surgically gloved hand towards the slab.

Moria stepped forwards reluctantly and groped around for ways to delay what must come. "I understand that self-installing augs are soon to be sanctioned."

Sylac grimaced. He glanced towards the autodoc, which drew back from the slab and hinged down, concealing all its glittering cutlery. Sylac had obviously instructed it to do this via his aug, perhaps to help put Moria at her ease.

"The early sensic augs were self-installing, until the first few deaths. Subsequently the investigating AI discovered that very few of the augs installed worked as they should—all failing to connect to all the requisite synapses. Some drove their owners into psychoses, others killed parts of their owners' brains."

"Is that what killed the ones who died?"

"In a sense. The nanofibre connections failed to untwine while being injected." Sylac shrugged. "Not much different from being stabbed through the head with a kebab skewer." Once again he gestured to the slab.

"And the improvement here?" Moria sat on the slab edge but was reluctant to lie down.

"Obviously I cannot guide every fibre to its synaptic connection. I guide trunks of fibres to the requisite areas of the brain and monitor the connection process, ready to intercede at any moment."

"Ah … that's good."

The nurse, who until then had been preoccupied at

something on one of the side work surfaces, came over to grip her biceps and firmly but gently ease her back. Moria couldn't really resist. That would be ridiculous. Already she had DNA marked, and had approved all the documentation and paid over the required sum. She must go with this now. Lifting her legs up onto the table she lay back, her neck coming down into a V-shaped rest and her head overhanging the end of the table where various clamps were ready to be engaged. The nurse began tightening these clamps as the autodoc rose beside Moria and flicked out one of its many appendages. Something stung at the base of her skull and suddenly everything above her neck felt dosed with anaesthetic. Her face and scalp felt like a rubbery bag hanging loose on her skull. Vision became dark-framed and hearing distant, divorced from reality.

In the tradition of medical practitioners throughout history, when putting a patient in a situation like this, Sylac said, "Wonderful weather we've been having lately, don't you think?" as if he expected some reply.

Moria waved a hand in lieu of replying in the affirmative or nodding her head. She heard the sound of the autodoc humming as it moved on its pedestal behind her. In the dark corners of her vision she could see those shiny limbs moving. Something tugged at the side of her head behind her ear. She heard suction, then the high-speed whine of a drill.

"One of the problems with those self-installing augs was first getting through the skull," Sylac observed.

Now there came a crunch.

"There, the bone anchors are in."

Moria would have preferred to have been unconscious throughout this procedure, but installing an aug to an unconscious brain was not possible, not yet. Now a cold feeling invaded her skull, and an ache grew behind her ear then quickly faded.

"Of course the weather we've been having has had its usual untoward effect, don't you think?" Sylac asked.

Again a wave of her hand.

"Connecting to the chiasma and optic tracts. You should shortly be experiencing optic division, or instatement of the 'third eye' as it is sometimes called."

The weirdest sensation ensued. With her vision tunnelling she became more aware of the fact that she gazed through two eyes—the separation became more defined—but now it seemed a lid had just opened on a third eye. It lay nowhere she could precisely locate, and though aware of its existence, she saw nothing through it. Very odd.

"That went well enough and now we are connecting to the cranial nerve. Raise your fist when the status text appears. And hereafter I want you to make a fist for yes and a flat hand for no."

Almost immediately after Sylac spoke, blue text appeared in the vision of her third eye: STATUS > and blinked intermittently. Moria raised her fist. Sylac continued talking, mentioning "occipital pole, frontal pole, basal ganglia, pons" and the only word Moria recognised, "cerebellum."

"Now visualize the words 'search mode' and affirm when the words appear."

Doing as instructed, Moria felt something engage inside her head. She suddenly realised she could visualize those words as normal, or she could make another connection that threw those words up in her third eye:

SEARCH MODE >

Moria raised her fist.

"I want you to think of something, anything to seek information upon. Input the words, then affirm—you will know how."

SEARCH MODE > AUBRON SYLAC

To begin the search Moria mentally spoke the word *go* and

sent it through the same channel as she sent the text.

NO NET CONNECTION. NO MEMSTORE.

"You have received two negatives for connection to the AI networks, and the internal storage of your aug?"

A fist.

"Good. Now we'll try something else. Try 'message mode.' "

MESSAGE MODE >

RECIPIENT >

MESSAGE >

ATTACH >

"I am in your address book. Send me something."

RECIPIENT > AUBRON SYLAC

MESSAGE > IS IT ALL AS SIMPLE AS THIS?

ATTACH > NIL

Go, Moria told it, and the text blinked out.

SENT.

"No, in doing this we are testing the connections. This is simple text. When you have run through the tutorial and become accustomed to your aug you'll find you can send messages in any informational form—that form merely limited by your imagination. And of course, sending messages is the least of your augmentation's functions."

Feeling suddenly returned to her face and scalp, and the world expanded around her. Her world continued to expand throughout the ensuing tests Sylac conducted. She ran complex equations, analysed data sent to her by Sylac, created specific programs and tailored search engines, learnt how to speak mind to mind, designed a very basic virtuality, discovered that through her aug she could actually alter how her body operated for through it she could take over autonomic functions. If she wished, she could stop her own heart. It was only the beginning, she at once understood, and immediately asked herself, *Why did I wait so long?*

"You are not yet connected to the AI grid, nor to the standard networks run by the planetary servers. That connection will be made after you have run the tutorial. As you were told, prior to installation, you need to give yourself at least two weeks to run that tutorial and become acclimatized."

Moria gazed at herself in the mirror beside the door to Sylac's surgery. The polished copper aug nestled neatly behind her left ear, complementing the copper scarab in her right earlobe. She pushed back her short, black hair and smiled at herself. After shaking Sylac's still-gloved hand, she took her leave. Stairs led down to the street door and out from air-conditioned asepsis into a muggy Trajeen evening.

One of Trajeen's three moons, Vina, hurtled across the sky in one of the five transits it made throughout the night. A second moon, Sutra, sat just above the horizon and Abhid had yet to rise. Beside Sylac's surgery, Moria's hydrocar awaited, but she decided to walk for a while. She didn't think it would be a good idea driving, even though her car was linked to city control and would be shut down if she did anything stupid. She decided to stroll to the centre of Copranus City and there enjoy a glass or two of greenwine to celebrate—Sylac had not warned her not to do anything like that.

On the street she noticed two examples of what Sylac had referred to as an untoward result of the clement weather they'd been experiencing. Two groundskate were hunching and flopping along the damp foam-stone, leaving slimy trails behind them. They were small examples—about a metre from wing tip to wing tip—but best avoided nonetheless. In themselves they weren't dangerous, but numerous people were injured each year after slipping on their trails, and sometimes if you got too close you ended up spattered with their slime.

Genfactored tulip trees lined the verges. They were in flower: yellow, blue and deep purple—the colours still evident in the fading light. In the street beyond Sylac's, jasmine hedges filled the air with a heavy, almost sickly perfume and, glancing beyond them, Moria observed microcosms of weird flora—genfactored and just plain alien. The houses behind these gardens were constructed of a local sandstone the colour of pine wood and similarly striated, their high-peaked roofs clad like lizard skin with shiny solar tiles. Bulbous chainglass windows occasionally revealed glimpses into luxurious homes, but then luxury was a standard in the Polity and people only lived impoverished lives as a matter of choice.

NET CONNECTION MADE

TUTORIAL LOADED >

Moria surveyed her surroundings, walked further until she came to a small park area in which a fountain cut cursive lines through the air above a wide pool containing giant lilies with flowers like purple claws, and shoals of small, blue flatfish in pellucid depths. All around her the scented air filled with the chirruping and occasional flutter of flying frogs. Finding a stone bench Moria seated herself and told her aug, *Go*.

VIRTUALITIES SELECT >

FANTASY REALMS

MODELLING REALITY

PREDICTION

EXPERIMENTAL

MANUFACTURING

The list scrolled endlessly down, but the tutorial chose the second on the list. Immediately, Moria found herself gazing into a blank white realm of infinite depth.

SELECT YOUR PLANETARY SYSTEM USING VOICE scrolled

across her vision. In her head spoke the words: *Trajeen planetary system—present moment.*

Starlit space filled the void, with the Trajeen system truncated to fit within her perception. She observed the planet she stood upon and the relative positions of the three moons around it—Vina being the only one visibly moving. The sun seemed close and she could see the arch of a solar flare. A quarter-orbit round and twice the distance from Trajeen as that planet was from the sun, the gas giant Boh lay tilted and swirled through with bands of blue, orange and yellow, seven of its eight moons hanging like steel ball bearings around it and the much larger moon, Tangie, with its internal living ocean packed full of exotic seaweeds, was a jade sphere coiled with pearly cloud.

SELECT CONSOLE AND CHOOSE CURSOR.

Console and square expandable cursor.

Numerous icons and virtuality controls sprang into being, framing her present view. The square that appeared at the centre of her vision moved with the motion of her third eye, though the view itself remained fixed. She brought it over to one of the icons and a text box appeared: THIS CONTROL ALTERS YOUR POV IN THE SYSTEM. Of course, when Moria began to try out the icon, with the prompting and frequent intercession of the tutorial program, she discovered it was nowhere near that simple. She could call up a three-dee map and place her point of view on that, she could input coordinates, she could whip through the planetary system as if aboard some craft travelling at any speed she chose, she could also select the time of this POV, moving back into recorded images—when available—or into modelling mode in both the past and future. Moving on to try out the endless layered icons and controls she realised there seemed nothing she could not do, she just needed to find out how. She could place objects in the system, track and alter vectors, play "what if" by moving a planet, moving anything, changing, reformatting, adding or taking away. She could work out how to bring about certain events and track back to reality to see the many scenarios that could bring them about. It was endless.

"Aug trance," someone said.

Briefly she surfaced into the real world and saw a woman stabbing a thumb at her as she and a man strolled past. Both of them wore augs themselves and the man grinned at her knowingly.

The tutorial took her on to explore applied mathematics, chemistry, though she sidelined the vast potential in organic chemistry with its programs for modelling genfactored life forms. Two hours later, with her neck stiff and the sky purple-black and flecked with stars above her, she paused the tutorial.

SUBCONSCIOUS LEARNING? > the tutorial program suggested. Finding out what that was about took her a further ten minutes. The tutorial could cycle at a level just below consciousness, almost like sleep-teaching. She chose that and stood. Walking then in a strange fugue in which she could interact with the real world around her while the tutorial played just at the edge of perception, she went to find those glasses of greenwine. In a bar in the city centre she chatted with two runcible technicians who recognised her from the Trajeen runcible project. When they headed off she found herself a niche and called up images of the two cargo runcible gates, one tracking a slow orbit about Trajeen itself and the other lying in orbit about Boh, the gas giant.

Thus far it had only been possible to transmit small objects through runcibles—nothing larger than a twenty-person shuttle—and mostly they were planet based and used to transport humans. Now over Trajeen and Boh they had built gates which, in theory, should be able to expand their Skaidon warps like the meniscus of a bubble. It should be possible to send through large spaceships, even asteroids should their ore value be worth the effort. The project received much criticism: Why transport large ships through a gate when such vessels could use their own underspace drives to enter that continuum anywhere? Why transport ore asteroids when they can be refined *in situ* and the product from them transported? Moria's answer to those who asked her such questions was always, why not?

RUNCIBLE TECHNOLOGY? > the tutorial suggested, and Moria lost herself for a further two hours. When she finally went to find her hydrocar and instructed it to take her home on automatic, she understood why it was necessary for her to take time off. Two more weeks of this, and by then she would have acquired the basics, the very basics.

The area beyond the armoured wall had been smashed by explosions and scoured by fire. The walls, floor and ceiling were torn apart, insulation bulged like moss from the rents, and power cables and fried optics hung sizzling. Some of the jags of metal protruding nearby still glowed red and kicked out oven heat, and smoke hung thick and acrid in the air. This all became more disorientating because no grav-plates were functioning here, and Jebel lost any perception of up and down. Urbanus paused for a moment, then abruptly stooped and flung Jebel over his shoulder. Jebel closed his eyes as the Golem began negotiating his way, fast, through the lethal chaotic jungle of hot metal and smoking plastic. At some point pain and blood loss impinged, and Jebel lost consciousness.

Hiatus.

"They just had to find out ... is that what you're saying?" said a woman.

"Yes, I think it must be," replied Urbanus.

Jebel opened his eyes and immediately felt a surge of nausea. He tried to keep it under control but spied a kidney dish containing a few pieces of bloody bone and a rind of flesh he realised must be his own. He leant over and puked, only then realising he lay on a surgical table. Glancing at his arm stump he saw that Urbanus had removed the biceps armour section and covered the raw end with an interface joint. But he felt better now, probably as a result of the contents of those empty synthetic-blood bags scattered on the floor, and whatever drugs Urbanus had pumped inside him. Now he focused on his companions.

"You survived," he managed.

Lindy Glick sat on the other surgical table in this small medbay. She had lost her translator gear and two of her front teeth, and a blue wound-dressing formed itself to the side of her skull. Jebel rather suspected that whatever mishap tore away the translator and damaged her mouth, had also torn her aug from the side of her head.

"Yeah, no thanks to our fucking AIs."

Jebel glanced at Urbanus. The Golem had lost syntheflesh all down his left-hand side. The metal of his upper arm, shoulder, side of his body, hip and upper leg lay exposed. He shrugged. "Don't look at me. I may be AI but I wasn't in charge of this shit-storm."

"'Sacrificial goat' I think is the old term." Lindy turned and spat out some blood. "They just had to put some people out there to find out how hostile these fuckers are." Now a boom echoed through the station, and Jebel surmised that the distant chattering clattering sounds he heard were from weapons fire. "I think they found out, don't you?" she added.

Jebel sat upright and swung his legs over the side of the table, watched for a moment while Urbanus placed some instrument against Lindy's upper mandible. He tried to aug into the station network but received only NO NET CONNECTION, and guessed that was due to some local security protocol. He cued a message for Cirrella to contact him the moment she could, since he guessed he would not be on time for dinner. Again he studied his arm stump. He was thinking his armour had not really served him very well until he turned his attention to the rest of his body.

His businesswear hung in tatters with one leg of his trousers burnt away. The composite armour underneath was scorched in many places and lumps of ceramal shrapnel were imbedded in his chest plate. Bearing in mind that he wore no head protection or gloves he considered himself lucky to have lost only an arm.

After a couple of sucking clicks, Urbanus extracted the instrument from Lindy's mouth, and stepped aside.

"How do they look?" she asked, exposing her two new teeth at Jebel.

"Lighter than your own, but better than the gap." He held up his stump. "I wouldn't mind the same."

Urbanus picked up a case, clicked it open and showed him the contents. "We don't really have the time to grow you a new one. This area has already been evacuated and we've been here too long. I'll fit it for you later. Now we must leave."

Jebel eyed the gleaming Golem lower arm and hand in the case as Urbanus snapped it closed. He pushed himself from the table, as Lindy did from hers, and they followed Urbanus to the door.

Something exploding much nearer shuddered the corridor as they entered it. He heard the sawing sounds of energy weapons of the kind that should never be used inside a space station, and wondered if they were being fired in defence or by the attackers.

"What about the others?" he asked.

"I believe seven of them made it out with the main crowd, though I cannot be sure of that," Urbanus replied.

Jebel felt a sick lurch in his stomach, but realised his reaction was muted by the antishock and analgesic drugs washing around inside him. Eighteen of his team dead, just like that, and fuck knows how many others killed in that chamber. What he wanted now was that arm attached so he could employ some lethal hardware. A proton carbine would do the trick, or maybe one of those nice compact missile launchers. He really felt the urge to make some crab paste.

Shortly they reached a drop-shaft that ran at an angle into the station body, but the irised gravity field was out—either damaged or shut down for security reasons. Urbanus peered up the shaft then turned to study Jebel.

"I will have to carry you."

"Can't you fit that arm now?"

"It would take too long."

Lindy led the way up the slanting ladder, Urbanus, with Jebel on his back, rapidly followed. As they left the shaft the depleted shock wave from an explosion below washed up past them. They traversed more corridors, one of them with its grav-plates malfunctioning, though luckily grav did not fluctuate above one standard gee. Finally they entered a wide boulevard lined with shops and residences, and a line of station forces awaited them: ceramal shields a metre thick raised up like lids on treaded vehicles, two portable flat-field generators, and behind these a row of tanks sporting missile launchers or particle cannons. The station security personnel were in full combat gear and Jebel saw that ECS forces also joined them. As he and the other two came to this line and were waved through, Jebel's aug informed him that net connection was reinstated—security procedure, then. His aug sent the cued message to Cirrella, and he set it to inform him the moment she contacted him.

Captain John Varence gazed out upon the firmament and knew it to be his home. He studied those points of light out there ... what were they ... stars ... and something niggled at his memory. Something about them, some connection, but he couldn't quite...

"*You are human,*" the other part of his consciousness reminded him. "*You were born on a planet called Earth orbiting a star called Sol.*"

No, that couldn't be right. Wasn't being human something to do with arms, legs and rather wet messy biology? He knew something about that, though was not entirely clear how he did know. Nothing to do with him. A fusion drive moved him omniscient and omnipotent near those glittery points, and U-space engines took him underneath the vastnesses between. He gazed out on it all with sensors capturing everything in the electromagnetic spectrum, felt the vacuum on his adamantine hull and bathed in the balm of hard radiation—his body, a massive, golden lozenge spined with sensor arrays, four kilometres long, one and a half wide and one deep. The body was his own for he felt the immediacy of all sensation within and at its skin. When damaged he suffered, when repaired he was healed. It stood under his utter control, its systems at his beck—

It was moving again...

Yes...yes he had decided to travel to those coordinates for he remembered starting the fusion engines with that other part of his mind. Why go there? Though omniscient, as part of the Polity, John served its purposes. And the Polity is the...

"*John, it is time—this ship is needed.*"

Some agreement with his other half, some contract made over a decade ago. He couldn't remember what that had all been about, though on some level there grew a tired acceptance.

U-space now, sinking into a somehow unreal continuum that came over only as grey to his multiple senses. The other made the calculations and the subtle alterations, it spoke with other entities of a similar kind, and now he could feel its steel-hard precision and something else there … sorrow.

"*Why am I sad?*"

"*Because evolution does not prepare its products for ending, and the finality of death can never be acceptable. I too, in a sense, am a product of evolution.*"

"*I know I am.*"

"*John…*"

Communication faded away from him, the grey he viewed reflected in his mind. Word and sensation blurred and lost meaning. Time passed. It does. A lurching twist snapped him out of reverie into the black and glitter of realspace.

"*What's that?*" he wondered.

"*The shipyard—our destination.*"

The *Occam Razor* drew in towards the spaceborne construction site, but being too massive to dock, held off a hundred kilometres. The structure was kilometres long, scaffolds spearing out into space, structural members like iron bones. Steely dots zipping around close seemed like flies around a corpse, but the shipyard was visibly growing under their ministrations. With childlike curiosity John Varence watched vessels smaller than himself heading over, docking themselves to his body, though he only vaguely recollected allowing that. Internally he watched those wetware creatures called humans coming aboard, and wondered what purpose they might serve.

"*I will be gentle,*" said the other.

John did not comprehend why he felt suddenly numb and that numbness seemed to be increasing. It was very strange, but he could no longer *feel* the fusion engines. The confusion did not last, within a minute he did not know what fusion engines were. The U-space drive was easier to forget, for he did not understand it anyway. He felt all his other senses somehow receding to a point inside his huge body—discomforts, a nagging ache and slight nausea localized there. Sensors, confined to a narrow part of the emitted spectrum between infrared and ultraviolet, came online within his larger body's bridge pod. He did not like them very much for they seemed dim and gummy, organic, even. Vacuum no longer touched his hull, rather air blew cool over febrile skin. No, he did not like this at all. Vision through his other senses remained and he forced a return to them, spying blackness again and vaguely familiar points of light.

"*What are they?*" he asked.

"*Stars, John,*" his other half replied.

All faded now to that central point as a solid scaffold of AI programming slowly withdrew. John shrank down into a shrivelled body on a throne, tugged and pushed slightly as optical and electrical connections detached and folded away.

"*Rest now,*" said the other.

John did not hear, already fading to a smaller and much stiller point in his ancient skull.

2.

So they took it away, and were married next day—

Newsnet services she auged into carried the same incredible comic-book stories. That all the newsnets seemed to be carrying the same story was probably one indication of the fault. Seated in her apartment, with her travel bag at her feet, Moria felt a clammy sweat grow on her body. The images she saw were just too cartoonish, too ridiculous, so the only explanation seemed to be that her aug was somehow scrambling up the newsnets with a fantasy virtuality. The programming of such a virtuality would certainly iron out inconsistencies and give the gloss of veracity to what she saw. She needed to do something about this before her brain ended up scrambled too.

MESSAGE MODE >

RECIPIENT > AUBRON SYLAC

MESSAGE > I NEED AN APPOINTMENT AT ONCE. MY AUG IS PRESENTING A FANTASY VIRTUALITY ON NEWSNET CHANNELS.

ATTACH > NIL

After a short delay she received the reply RECIPIENT NOT FOUND which seemed to confirm that her aug was malfunctioning. But what to do? She was due on a shuttle flight back to the Trajeen runcible complex in two hours. Should she just head over to Sylac's surgery first and hope he could do something in the limited time? No, she would have to try to put this right herself.

OFFLINE NETLINK>

WARNING: SERVER STORED INFORMATION WILL BE LOST.

WARNING: COMLINK BOOT CODES—

With a grimace Moria input her instruction: OFFLINE NETLINK> CONFIRM.

It seemed, suddenly, as if a silence fell inside her head.

MEMSTORE> DELETE

CONFIRM?> YES

YOU ARE COMPLETELY SURE YOU WANT TO DELETE YOUR MEMSTORE?> YES!

REPEAT MEMSTORE DELETE X3> DELETE DELETE DELETE

CONFIRM> YES!!!

MEMSTORE DELETED.

That took care of anything nasty she might have picked up via her netlink, which was not unheard of.

DIAGNOSTIC> RUN FROM PARTITION SIX, THEN REPEAT IN DESCENDING ORDER FROM EACH OTHER PARTITION.

DIAGNOSTIC RUNNING—ONE HOUR TO COMPLETION.

Moria sighed—this at least would track down any bugs in the aug, unless of course there was also something wrong with the diagnostic program. The time delay also wiped the idea of going to visit Sylac before heading for her shuttle, since he would be unable to do anything while the diagnostic ran. Now she had an hour to kill before driving to the shuttle port, which was only ten minutes away. She stood and walked into her kitchenette, drew off a cup of tea from her hot drinks dispenser—obstinately ignoring the bottle of greenwine open on the counter—then returned to her living room.

Leaning back in her chair she felt it adjust for her comfort. But comfort did not seem enough for she immediately began to miss her aug. Sipping her tea she looked around for something to occupy her mind, and her gaze fell on the remote control for the holoprojector lying on the chair's side table. Eyeing it she noticed the dust on its controls, for since Sylac installed her aug she had felt no need to use her holoprojector. Picking up the remote, and observing the imprint it left on the table, she frowned, and punched in the number for the building submind.

Hovering just a couple of metres from her face, a black hole appeared. Out of this scuttled a large rat to squat upright in midair. "Moria Salem?" it enquired, tilting its head. Why the building's submind chose to represent itself as such had always been a matter of debate among some of the residents. Moria did not think there was much to discuss—like many AIs it simply possessed a distorted sense of humour.

"My cleanbot doesn't seem to be doing its job," she told it.

The rat looked over to one side as if inspecting something, then replied, "That's because you recently transferred the controls of your apartment from this unit to your new aug, and failed to input instructions." The rat shrugged. "I could have done something about this, but we AIs much prefer it when humans try to use their own brains."

"Er ... thank you," said Moria, "that's all."

The rat turned and scurried back into its hole and the hole snapped shut. Moria grimaced, since there was nothing she could do now while the diagnostic ran. Instead she punched in the number for the newsnet service she used before obtaining her aug, and recently used via her aug. Time now to find out what was really going on in the world.

The huge multi-legged monster rose out of the floor before her, claws spread and mandibles grating over her head. Black holographic saliva dribbled down upon her body.

"Aaah!" Moria flung herself from her chair and was

backing away on her knees before she started to feel really foolish.

"This creature, this Vortex," the announcer was saying, "could be a different species, larger kin, or perhaps just a differently developed version of the same species as is a soldier ant in a nest of ants."

Moria tuned the rest out because she had already heard it via her aug. In the subsequent hour she learnt from simple screen links to friends and associates and by scanning all the newsnet services that no, her aug had not malfunctioned, and yes, big exoskeletal hostile aliens were attacking the Polity, *and* the fuckers ate people.

The antishock drugs and analgesics were beginning to wear off, but Jebel did not ask for any more since there were others in this medical unit with a greater need, and he wanted his mind to remain clear while auged into the station network, and while he watched through its camera eyes.

Docked to the ship like some huge golden parasite, the Prador shuttle yet showed no sign of departing, and the station AI wanted to do something about that. Through exterior cams, when the bandwidth could be spared, Jebel observed a pan-pipes missile launcher squirting its load out into space. No point tracking them, so he focused back on the shuttle. The missiles returned too fast to be seen, and the flash of the silent impacts blanked vision for a moment. Fire rolled across the station skin, and Jebel grabbed the head frame of the cot he sat upon as the medical unit shuddered all around him. As the view cleared he saw the disheartening reality: the shuttle remained untouched. Now linking in and picking up what he could of AI.com to ships beyond the station, he understood that the weaponry required to destroy the shuttle might destroy the station itself. AI minds then discussed the idea of slicing through the station to remove this alien tick. But it was not the resultant loss of human life that scotched the idea. Quite simply, though a Prador attack force operated from the shuttle, that vessel might be all that prevented the mother ship from attacking, and against that they could mount little defence.

"How are you?"

Jebel saw Urbanus enter the medical unit, but only now turned his full attention to the Golem. "Sick and in pain."

"Well that won't last—you're going into surgery now. Any personnel with combat training get priority."

"That makes me feel all warm inside."

"Come on." Urbanus tossed him a drug patch, which Jebel peeled and stuck on the side of his neck. As he pushed himself from the cot he experienced a momentary dizziness and found his missing hand begin to ache. Seconds later the patch's contents did their work and he felt suddenly euphoric.

"What's happening?" Jebel asked. "I just watched the AI try to take out the shuttle, but aug com inside the station is censored when it isn't going down."

"About a hundred of them have penetrated the station and cut off the section between the Green Transept Arcade and the Delta rim locks. People are escaping via the runcible within that area, but that cannot last."

Despite the drugs, Jebel's guts knotted up. Cirrella's apartment lay within that area. "What … cannot last?"

Remorselessly Urbanus replied, "The AI will have to destroy the runcible to prevent it falling into Prador… claws."

Jebel's nausea returned, but what else could the AI do? What could Jebel do in his present condition? He needed to return himself to fighting fitness to help her.

They exited the medical unit into a corridor busy with station personnel, many of them guiding grav-sleds stacked with munitions. Towards the end of this corridor he saw another packed full of civilians slowly edging their way along it. Many of them carried small holdalls or other items.

"From the area they took?" Jebel suggested.

"No, evacuation. All the runcibles are open port and the AI is getting people out as fast as it can." He glanced at Jebel. "ECS dreadnoughts out there. You know what will probably happen when they engage that Prador mother ship, and there seems little doubt that they will."

Jebel understood: a station, in close proximity to whatever battle ensued, would be highly vulnerable—a liability. That did not, however, make him feel any better about it.

A row of med bays lay just down from the unit. Urbanus drew to a halt before one door, stood gazing at it for a moment, then stepped aside pushing Jebel back. The door opened and an auto-stretcher planed out—the woman upon it unconscious and clad head to foot in one of those tight suits Jebel recognised as the kind normally worn after major skin replacement. Urbanus guided him through the door to where two med-techs oversaw five surgical slabs and five menacing autodocs. Three of the slabs were occupied and on one of them a vaguely human figure was being tugged about by two of the docs. Jebel spied shattered ribs splayed out, blood-filled tubes and a lung inflating, legs gone at the knee and charred, weeping skin. The rest was a blur of gleaming appendages, the low droning of bone and cell welders, hissing, sucking and crunching sounds. He directed his gaze elsewhere.

"This is him?" asked a thin, blonde-haired woman who poised over another autodoc, reprogramming it. She shot a glance at his missing arm. "Yes, I see it is." Turning, she picked up the case Urbanus had brought from the other med bay, opened this and took out the Golem hand and forearm. "Up on the slab."

Jebel hesitated, feeling this was going too quickly.

"On the slab now!" the woman bellowed. "I've people dying out there!"

Jebel obeyed, guilty because his wound could have waited, and because he was receiving treatment ahead of others in greater need. And why? Because he had been trained in causing precisely the kind of injuries this woman must now treat. He lay back, felt the nerve blocker go into his neck without further delay, and his body turn into a numb piece of steak from below there. Then the autodoc whirred into place over his arm stump as if preparing to dine. Jebel closed his eyes.

Moria gazed up at what was now a familiar image to her, this time appearing on the public screen aboard the shuttle taking her back to the Trajeen cargo runcible: the big Prador chopping the human ambassador in half. Now the presenters were waxing lyrical in reference to this attack on the Polity's *Avalon* as that story slowly began to be displaced by stories of other attacks.

"Well," said Carolan Prentis, from the seat beside her, "xenobiologists have been crying about the lack of sentient aliens we've encountered. I wonder how they feel now?"

Still feeling a little shaken, and thoroughly annoyed with herself, Moria glanced at her companion. Carolan wore her blue runcible-technician overall with the same pride as Moria, though her project ranking was lower. Her elfin face, which was undoubtedly the product of cosmetic surgery, reminded Moria of something out of a VR fantasy game (Moria grimaced at the analogy—who was she to know the difference between fantasy and reality?), though Carolan's dark brown eyes with their green flecks and her incongruous cropped blonde hair seemed likely to be the product of genetics. Undoubtedly some ancestor of Carolan's had undergone genetic redesign, for on each wrist a wheel tattoo overlaid scars where spur fingers had been excised.

Moria turned away, gazing internally as her aug—now with the diagnostic finished and her netlink re-established—loaded information from various searches and began rebuilding programs she had earlier deleted. It surprised her to find this woman on the same shuttle as herself. Her surprise doubled to see Carolan now wore an aug too—coincidentally having visited Copranus City for a fitting at the same time.

She turned back towards Carolan. "It probably depends on how close they are to all this." Moria nodded at the screen, now displaying a shot of a moon installation being bombed by one of those horribly massive ships. "I bet they're coming in their pants back on Earth, but out closer to the line they might be a little less happy about it all."

"Mmm, I guess ... you know they've been discussing mining the cargo gate?"

"What?"

"Well, we're not that far from the line here and they don't want these Prador getting hold of runcible tech."

"But they don't have AIs."

"Nevertheless..."

Moria thought about those words, *we're not that far from the line here*, but though she understood on an intellectual level what the newsnets were displaying, she could not quite equate it with the reality she knew.

The shuttle, a fifty-metre cylinder with a rounded nose and two stubby wings, rose steadily on AG, and the fusion flame of its main engine drove it through the Trajeen atmosphere. Moria always preferred this particular shuttle over the more usual delta-wings because of its ample provision of windows. She gazed out at the falling curve of the planet and the gradual winking on of stars in the purple-black firmament.

The moon Abhid lay within view to the fore of the shuttle, but Vina and Sutra were not visible. Modelling the planetary system in her aug she realised Sutra would soon be coming into view over the horizon, just below and down at four o'clock from Abhid. Vina, presently lying over on the other side of Trajeen, would only be visible to the rear of the shuttle just before it docked at the cargo gate. Vina's position influenced the timing of shuttle launches, since thus far the fast-moving moon had eaten up one public shuttle and two private vessels. Miscalculate the position of something two hundred kilometres across and travelling at 40,000 kph and you won't get any second chances. Just as an exercise to distract her from what the screen was showing she ran statistical calculations on the chances of ending up in the moon's path, considering the number of launches from the planet over the last twenty years, and the navigational and computer systems available to those craft. She then calculated escape vectors and drive thrust requirements, swiftly realising that those aboard the three craft, whose remains lay impacted on Vina's surface, had been rather unlucky.

Again to keep herself distracted from some particularly nasty images now being displayed, Moria began an investigation into the circumstances surrounding those shuttle crashes, and immediately stumbled on some conspiracy theory net sites. According to them, one of the privately owned craft belonged to someone who later turned out to be a chief financier of Separatist terrorists on Trajeen. And the other belonged to an out-Polity weapons dealer. The AIs killed them, the theorists claimed. While she studied circumstances surrounding the crash of the public shuttle, Sutra rose as predicted, and she snorted with satisfaction.

"You were running something in your aug," said Carolan

Moria turned to her. "Is it so obvious?"

"As with me. I'm told we'll only develop the ability to compartmentalize after a few months of usage. What were you running?"

Moria did not like the question. It almost seemed equivalent to, "What are you thinking?" As she understood it, the behavioural ethos slowly being established for aug usage was that you did not ask such questions unless they were work related. She answered anyway.

"That's pretty damned advanced," Carolan replied with a puzzled frown. "I haven't even started on that level of modelling and calculus. Where did you have your aug fitted?"

"Privately—a surgeon by the name of Aubron Sylac."

"You didn't use an ECS-approved clinic?"

"No."

"Oh."

Moria sank back into a trancelike state, and after quickly working through the theories concerning the shuttle crash, dismissed them all and began working on her own. Calling up the specs of that shuttle, maintenance record, component failures, available backgrounds on pilot and passengers, she began to put together various scenarios. Abruptly she found the compass of her perception expanding as she began grabbing information from the local server and AI net. She realised that suddenly she was, as Carolan described it, compartmentalizing, because now she remained thoroughly aware of her physical surroundings, even while running searches and calculations. With a sudden surge of excitement she abruptly comprehended the sheer extent of what she was doing, the intricacy of detail, the incredible logic chains. Swiftly and precisely she came to her conclusion. The shuttle had been sabotaged. Someone broke the security protocols of its control systems and caused a course change resulting in it falling in the path of Vina.

Abruptly: NO NET NO NET *&?@??

What the hell?

"You are, of course, entirely correct, but no one must know about this," spoke a voice in her head.

"Who is this?"

Her aug supplied the answer: IDENTIFIER: TRAJEEN SYSTEM CARGO RUNCIBLE AI.

"Oh shit."

Moria felt sweat break out all over her body.

"You will not post this information, and I advise that you delete it from your augmentation's memstore."

"Erm…"

"The matter was resolved. Consider: the two private vessels contained those with Separatist affiliations. They crashed into Vina after the shuttle … accident. You'll not require further net access to understand the course of events."

Moria immediately replied, *"They caused the shuttle crash. It was an act of terrorism and they were … executed?"*

"Outstanding. Now, Carolan Prentis has sent you her eddress. I suggest, when I reconnect you, that you reply to her and study the information she has found. We will talk further after your shuttle docks. Again: do not attempt to post what you have discovered."

NET CONNECTION MADE >

EDDRESS REQUEST >

OFFLINE EDDRESS REQUEST?

ACCEPT?

Moria accepted, and shortly afterwards received an information package from Carolan Prentis:

Aubron Sylac (neuro-interface development, cosmetic, mechano and cerebral augmentation surgeon, MD of Anosin Cyberoptics, Professor of biomechanics, cerebral dynamics, nanobiotics and submicron mechanics, AI Philosophy and Synaptic Programming) was rumoured to have arrived on Trajeen this week. Three solstan years ago he escaped from Adjustment in the main clinic in London, Britain, on Earth, and ECS agents have been pursuing him ever since.

—Oh fuck—

Aubron Sylac was sentenced to Adjustment for illegal and dangerous research into augmentation technology…

—Double fuck—

The walls were seemingly constructed of laminated layers of rough white stone, green and red stained with algae. Tangles of iron-grey weed sprouted in crevices and large glistening lice scuttled here and there. In the ceiling, large metal grids concealed the slow rotation of fans which drew damp oceanic air through. The floor was pitted and scratched by the passage of hard spiky feet. Within this cavelike sanctum Captain Immanence, an adult Prador whose carapace spanned five metres, studied the fractured displays in the array of hexagonal screens before him and felt thoroughly satisfied with present progress. Sliding on the AG units shell-welded to the underside of his carapace he turned slowly towards the two second-children who had recently entered.

"Feed me," he commanded.

The two children scuttled forwards dragging the dripping purple slab of a mega fauna steak between them. Once directly below his mandibles they began tearing it apart and passing it up to him, piece by piece. Immanence still retained one claw and two legs, which was a bonus at his great age—only adolescent Prador retained the ability to regrow limbs—but preferred to be fed like this. It was a way of asserting authority and he knew that having to do this terrified both first-, second- and third-children alike, for there was no telling when he might feel inclined to eat one of them. Of course, they were thoroughly under the control of his pheromonal emissions, but the additional fear tended to make them even more solicitous of his good opinion.

As he munched his steak, scattering bloody gobbets on the floor to be scavenged by the ship lice, he considered Vortex's earlier message. It seemed that human flesh did not taste bad at all, and that there might be further benefits in subjugating this soft and complacent species. He finished the meat and allowed one of the second-children to scrub the resultant mess from his mandibles then polish them back to their usual sheen. While this task was being conducted he widened the channel connecting him, via one of the five control units welded to his carapace underneath his remaining claw, to the choud operating the controls behind him, and instructed it to move the ship closer to *Avalon Station*. Next, his mandibles gleaming sufficiently, he spun back to the controls and screens.

The two chouds here in the sanctum were hunched over, their branching forelimbs deep in pit controls and actually nerve-connected into the ship's hardware. The creatures, with their shiny hemispherical heads and segmented bodies, bore some similarity to ship lice, and were in fact related. Immanence noted that one of them was developing those grey patches that indicated its imminent demise. He controlled his irritation. Another would have to be brought up from storage, cored and thralled, and then installed. Elsewhere in the ship other creatures from home-world were similarly cored and thralled—their inadequate main ganglions removed and replaced by Prador thrall hardware—and ran the vessel's critical systems. Some of them would no doubt also die soon. Immanence preferred to use this method of controlling his ship because the creatures acted as a buffer between himself and the ship's systems. Direct connection via his control units would leave him vulnerable to attack by some rival. But it was not an ideal situation. Immanence realised that now, though he would not have given it a second thought a hundred years ago. It was the humans that showed how much better things could be: their dextrous and sensitive hands, their senses almost on a par with that of the Prador themselves, those small bodies capable of worming their way into any niche. To thrall and control such creatures would offer untold advantages to the Prador. And the fact that you could eat them as well…

Immanence hissed and bubbled. Unfortunately, the few human captives provided by human agents outside the Polity proved too weak to survive the process—the slightest injury seemed to kill them; the ability to survive the loss of a leg, or of bodily fluids, or withstand pain seemed non-existent. Cutting open their skulls and removing the higher cerebrum killed them instantly unless certain elaborate precautions were taken. But if they did survive that, the nerves died at the thrall connection points and then some infection took hold and quickly finished them off. This was not an insuperable problem. Prador researchers just needed more subjects for experimentation, so crushing this Polity seemed to be all benefit.

Now studying the screens before him, Immanence saw that two of the five human vessels here were moving between his own ship and the station. He again ran scans on them to confirm the incredible facts: yes, these ships were large, fast and well-armed, but their layered outer hulls consisted of weak composites and superconducting grids. Only one of them carried a layer of armour Immanence deemed of any note—this consisting of some form of ceramal. Perhaps this all came down to the psychological dissimilarities between the two species: for Prador, after all, armour was integral to their psyche.

"Vortex, report," Immanence instructed.

Two of the hexagonal screens showed views from cameras mounted on that first-child's carapace, whilst an anosmophone filled the air about Immanence with the smells from the station. He detected the complex odours of things burning, the perfumes of various alien plants, hot circuitry, ozone generated by energy weapons fired in an oxygen atmosphere. These smells were, on the whole, familiar to the captain. But the smell generated by humans living in close confinement, the tang from ripped human bodies, and the pheromonal reek of their fear were new and most interesting to him.

"We have approximately nine hundred prisoners ready to take aboard the shuttle. Our casualties stand at thirty-eight per cent. Human forces—brought in from elsewhere in the Polity by their matter transmission devices—are increasing outside the encirclement. I estimate that they will penetrate our line within the hour," Vortex replied.

"You have maintained the gap between your forces and their runcible?"

"I have, but we are losing potential captives through there."

"Necessary, Vortex—they would only destroy it if you got too close, either that or cease evacuating and start bringing forces in through there."

Immanence called up the views from the cameras in the hold aboard the shuttle docked with the station. He observed humans packed tight in one of the four small holds, and listened to the curious noises they were making. The pheromonal reek of fear rose even stronger from there.

"Retreat to the shuttle now," Immanence instructed. "We don't know what other forces they might bring in, and I feel we have sufficient subjects for the present. Once you are aboard, seal the airlocks and await instructions."

Now the Prador captain returned his attention to the

Polity battleships, whilst fully linking to the second choud which ran his own ship's weapons systems. Calling up a multiple screen image of the ship he selected, one of those lying between his own and the station, he paused to study its layout. The vessel was vaguely triangular, with balanced U-space engine nacelles protruding to its rear. Immanence's weapon of choice in this instance was one of the particle cannons. With a thought, he gave the choud its instructions.

The turquoise beam of field-accelerated metal ions whipped out towards the Polity ship. The vessel instantly began to accelerate and returned fire with high-intensity gas lasers. Immanence noted the more distant ships launching swarms of missiles, while those closer began moving in to engage with energy weapons. The particle beam tracked down along the length of the Polity ship, mostly deflected by hard-fields, but the captain observed satisfying explosions within the vessel as hard-field generators overloaded. When the beam played back past the engines, it stabbed on momentarily to punch a hole in the station. Fire tracked escaping air out into vacuum from a glowing crater there.

Immanence observed the negligible effects of the laser strikes on his own ship. The exotic metal armour reflected most of the energy, but that remaining by conduction was hardly enough to warm up the heat distributing s-con grid. He analysed his attack on the Polity ship and ascertained weaknesses, then, with lazy insouciance, cut the vessel in half.

His own defence lasers began firing automatically on the approaching missile swarm. Seeing that the missiles were employing some kind of antimunitions to baffle targeting sensors, he switched to wide-beam masers and watched one or two explosions, but mostly saw missiles glow bright then go out like embers. But inevitably, some got through.

Detonation.

Immanence analysed the explosion caused by some form of fission weapon. A second and a third followed immediately, and through outside sensors he observed atomic fire spewing into space. Within his sanctum he felt the ship dip and shudder. But the explosions were well within parameters. The s-con grid drew heat away to thermal generators, topping off the vessel's energy supplies. The piezoelectric layers in the exotic metal armour also complemented that charge. The ship's laminar batteries swiftly rose to repletion, and winding up the power to all four particle cannons, Immanence fired on the second ship lying between him and the station. That vessel turned nose-on to reduce its target area and switched over to masers. The four turquoise beams converged on its nose, incidentally punching more holes into the station behind during their transit. Shield generators held out for a few seconds, then the strike gutted the ship from nose to stern. Something inside then detonated to spread clouds of glowing debris and incandescent gas.

The Prador captain swung his ship around and began accelerating towards the other vessels. More impacts on his hull, and a steady rise in temperature from maser strikes.

"The more you hit me, the stronger I get," Immanence sang.

Now he began launching some of his own missiles, then watched with steadily growing annoyance how they were destroyed. This must to be due to those artificial intelligences the humans used, no Prador vessel could have reacted so fast and decoded the various methods of concealment the missiles used. The Polity possessed an advantage when it came to handling information, but what matter? Brute force always won out in the end.

Immanence fired his particle beams at the armoured

Polity vessel. This spherical ship was obviously of a more modern design, it being larger than the others and its U-space drive evidently inside. The ship absorbed fire and fell back, glowing lines etched across its hull and finally fading. It came on again, and this time when Immanence fired upon it, the particle beams veered and dispersed. The ship had obviously given its hull a huge negative charge to counter the negatively charged ion beams. Immanence ramped up the acceleration towards it, turning his particle cannons towards the other two ships which where firing on him from either side. The armoured Polity ship also accelerated.

Interesting, thought Immanence, *are those aboard prepared to sacrifice themselves to stop me?*

Something else now began to strike his ship. Analysing the data, the captain realised the other vessel had begun firing some form of particle cannon, one that delivered its energy in high-powered pulses. This weapon had obviously been designed to overload the heat dispersal properties of an s-con grid. It did not work, of course, for the exotic armour reacted inversely, converting the excess energy to mechanical movement, realigning its crystalline structure and in fact straightening out some recent dents. Other energy excesses Immanence again discharged through all four particle cannons at once. One of the other ships fell away, fires lighting it internally, and one sliced-off U-space nacelle tumbling in vacuum behind it.

The armoured vessel drew close and showed no sign of diverting from its course. Scan returns showed its hull still negatively charged for repelling an anion particle beam. Amusing, really. Immanence noted the net charge of his own vessel to be highly positive, enough so that there was a measurable attraction between the two ships. He redirected his particle cannons, but not sure how efficient was the other ship's scanning gear, he waited until the last moment before inverting the cannons' charge output. He fired that four-fold blast, this time the beams consisting of cations. There followed a massive impact, as Immanence's vessel struck burning wreckage, mostly. The impact jolted him down to the floor, but he rose smoothly again as he turned his ship to seek out the remaining Polity vessel. Sensibly it accelerated away and soon dropped itself into U-space. As he returned towards the station, Immanence ran diagnostics to check his own ship for damage. There was some, but not enough to concern him. Clattering his mandibles in Prador laughter he reckoned this war would be an endless source of pleasure for him.

Standing at the junction of four corridors, Jebel flexed his gleaming fingers and touched their tips together, amazed at the illusion of sensation he felt. The ceramal fingertips possessed no artificial nerves, but pressure sensors in each intricately constructed joint partially served the same purpose. However, when he swapped his weapon to that hand, the difference became evident. Despite the knurled inner faces to his new fingers, thumb and palm, his grip was lacking but it would have to serve. He glanced across at Urbanus, who slung his proton carbine by its strap across one shoulder and presently strapped on a grenade belt. The sensitivity of the Golem's touch being enhanced by his covering of syntheflesh and syntheskin, he suffered no such disadvantages. Lindy, though a trained ECS monitor, had been seconded elsewhere because of her linguistic speciality. Besides, she had not been instructed in the disciplines required here: zero-gee orientation and combat. Jebel returned his attention to the weapon he held and grinned. The hand-held missile launcher sported a fifty-shot ring magazine, and two further magazines nestled in the pack strapped to his back.

"Some of you have already been in fire fights, the rest of you listen hard: these fuckers carry a lot of firepower and they do not die easily," said the Sparkind placed in charge of them. "Take off a man's arm," she shot a glance at Jebel, "and he's out of play for a while. I saw one of them stripped down to its carapace only, yet it still managed to bite off the foot of someone who stepped too close. Be warned."

Helen, the Sparkind, was a tough-looking woman with either snakeform cosmetic alteration or full ophidaption—her skin glinted with small scales and whenever she got a bit excited her fangs dropped into biting position. She became slightly aerated when told to take command of those from station security and the ECS regulars who were experienced in zero-gee combat. The other three members of her Sparkind unit—a man and two state-of-the-art Golem—had been placed in command of other groups. It was a necessary adaptation to circumstances, now that the Prador had cut the power to the grav-plates in the area they controlled. The area where Cirrella's apartment lay.

She continued: "The pincams are all out and the Prador are jamming scan. Our augs won't function there either and com is limited. We go in, kill anything in a shell, and reinstate cams and grav so the backup teams can follow." She surveyed the group, noting the rank badges of each individual. "You ECS regulars, you know what to do. Take corridors 12A and B and go through to the meeting point. You have to check accommodation units, as the smaller Prador can get through the doors. And check your targets. There are still people hiding in there—any you find, send them back this way." The four station security personnel she sent through the hydroponics tube, perhaps the easier option, if any option could be so designated. Now she turned to Jebel, Urbanus, and the five ECS monitors Jebel had selected from his own surviving personnel. "You're with me—we go through the factory."

The other units headed away to their entry points, while Helen led the way to the access stairs down into an autofactory.

"You, Urbanus, will take first lead with me, along with you two." She stabbed a finger alternately at two of Jebel's men. "The plates are operating on this side of the factory so until we hit the nil-gee area we use simple four-by-four cover." Helen glanced at Jebel. "I intend to run a search pattern through there, so we won't be going in a straight line to the other side. I do not want one of those bastards behind us. When we hit nil gee we go to an axis advance: one by the floor, one by the ceiling, and the other two left and right. Any questions?"

Jebel guessed she had it covered. He glanced at one of his personnel, Jean Klars, who carried a heavy rail-gun. She crossed her eyes at him and stuck out her tongue. He guessed Sparkind possessed more respect for their commanders, though his own people were a good bunch and shouldn't fuck up.

The stair ended at a corridor, one side glassed, running above the end of the factory. Emergency lights lit the place, and Jebel glimpsed the nightmare machine jungle before Helen signalled them to get down. They crawled below the long window, then came upright again beyond it while Helen gazed pensively down another stair to a single door.

"They'll probably have that covered," Jebel noted, perhaps stating the obvious.

"Com check," Helen said, her voice also audible in Jebel's earpiece. She gestured back to the chainglass window and took a small decoder mine from her belt. "Six metre drop. I'm okay with that and, of course, so is Urbanus. We'll go that way, and I'll let you know when the rest of you can use the door."

Jean glanced at Jebel and raised an eyebrow. He shrugged in reply. Obviously these Sparkind were trained to a level he'd never encountered before. He did not know of any humans, even boosted, who could take a six metre drop in their stride.

Helen slapped the decoder mine against the glass. Immediately it activated, initiating the disintegration of the molecular chains in the glass. The entire window turned white, crazed, then collapsed into a falling curtain of glittery powder. Helen vaulted through, swiftly followed by Urbanus. He heard a muffled "Bollocks" from below and made a slight reassessment of Helen's superhuman abilities. Minutes dragged by, then, "Okay, you're clear."

They moved quickly down the stairs, the first two covering the rest as they moved into the shut-down factory. Helen took her three to the first monolithic machine—an enormous powder forge—then moved on to track along beside a conveyer. Jebel brought his three to the forge and they took up cover positions. And so it continued through aisles between moulding machines with micrometrically adjustable moulds, more conveyors, rollers, presses, welding and general-purpose assembler robots. As they moved it became necessary to scan and cover much above floor level as well, because this factory's production lines did not only run in two dimensions. That half the grav-plates were active in here was unusual as such factories were normally zero gee with the machines working in three dimensions. A cage-work extended from floor to ceiling, supporting further machines, robots, conveyers, all the panoply of high-tech, high-speed production. Entering such a place when it was in operation would not have been a clever idea. The AI running it would obviously try to avoid causing you injury, but you might get in the way of some process it just could not stop in time, and you'd get ground up in the cogs.

Halfway across the alloy floor, Helen was one moment walking, then she launched herself into the air, diving upwards to thump against an extruder caught mid-belch of rows of coppery pipes. Urbanus remained at floor level while the other two jumped up and to either side to roughly form the axis pattern Helen required of them as they advanced. When Jebel reached the deactivated grav-plates, he signalled for Jean Klars to remain at floor level, the other two to take the sides, while he launched himself for the ceiling. Almost the moment he stopped himself against the underside of a large crane arm, the firing started.

The hideous racket of a projectile stream slamming against machinery sent most of them ducking for cover, but the ricochets all about made it difficult to locate the source. Jebel thought himself hit, blood and gobbets of flesh spattered him. A laser also fired, the beam not visible except where it struck. Flashes lit the entire factory as if someone were using an arc welder. As he pulled himself up behind the thicker part of the arm, Jebel saw one of those with Helen, tumbling through the air with smoke belching from his body. He bounced against the side of a multipress, scattering blackened pieces, then burst into flame. Jebel felt vulnerable where he hung—not enough metal between himself and whatever lay ahead of them. He pushed off from the arm, coiling himself in a ball while he flew across the gap between the arm and some bulbous furnace. The snap-crack of a laser tracked him, and he pulled himself to cover with a leg of his fatigues smouldering.

"Our commander is no longer with us," said Urbanus over com.

Jebel realised that now—he saw Helen's remains floating up by the ceiling. "Have you got that bastard spotted?"

"*Those* bastards, I suspect," the Golem replied.

Jebel took a quick look at the masses of machinery ahead,

then ducked back. By his estimation, the one with the laser hid behind an automated milling machine down on the floor to his left.

"Covering fire," he ordered, then, upside down, crawled down the face of the furnace until he obtained a better view from underneath it. The racket of weapons fire and the stink of burning filled the air. Movement behind the mill—confirmation. He fired five explosive missiles. Out of the explosion leapt a Prador, bouncing acrobatically from machine to machine. They hit it three or four times, but it did not slow. Of course, with that number of limbs it was much better in AG than humans, and could afford to lose a few. The creature darted between two heavy powder forges.

"All of you but Jean target the other side of those two forges. Jean, concentrated burst this side—just don't stop firing."

The rail-gun Jean wielded filled the gap between the two machines with a hornet swarm of lethal ricochets and ceramal shrapnel. The Prador hurtled from the other side to avoid this hail. It trailed smoke in the convergence of fire from the others and Jebel enjoyed the satisfaction of seeing three of his missiles slam home. The creature flew apart. Jebel observed one leg stuck to a metal surface nearby, still quivering. Then the second Prador appeared, leaping a gap. Urbanus used the launcher facility on his carbine, pumping grenade after grenade up through a narrow gap from his position below. The Prador tried to jump clear of them but went straight into the convergence of laser strikes. It issued a bubbling shriek, struck the side of a conveyer and tumbled out into the open. Some of its limbs burst open, smoke and flame wreathed it as the concentrated fire did not let up. Jebel aimed to deliver the *coup de grâce*, but then put up his weapon. The others continued to fry the creature.

Its bubbling screams continued for about a minute—a very long time in such a situation. Eventually it drifted against a wall and tried to pull itself to cover. Only then did Jebel fire his missile launcher, blowing the creature to smoking fragments.

The acrid burnt-fish stink filling the air made him gag. It never occurred to him that he would become accustomed to this odour.

Performed at appallingly fast AI speeds, the weapons refit took only two days, and now the *Occam Razor* stood ready to engage the enemy. However, the idea of updating the rest of the old dreadnought's antiquated systems was abandoned, for it would have taken much longer to do that than turn out an entirely new dreadnought from the production line. The *Occam Razor* had been built a century or so before when humans ruled and AIs were considered untrustworthy slaves, consequently Occam, the ship's AI, had been built as an adjunct to an interfaced captain who was capable of initiating a system burn to destroy the AI should it get out of control.

Captain Varence, some years before, passed into senescence as a result of his ancient implants decaying and spreading toxic chemicals throughout his body, and because in the end he became old and tired of life. From then, Occam steadily assumed greater control of the ship while the captain faded, and for the steady functioning of the vessel in peace time this was no problem, since during this time it was only used as a passenger and cargo vessel. ECS now required the *Occam Razor,* the biggest battleship the Polity owned, to be fully functional: capable of reacting at speed, but most importantly, of using its weapons. But the hard-wiring originally installed did not allow for the AI to use the weapons without the approval of its interfaced captain.

And in those last years Varence had been incapable of giving his approval to very much at all, and tended to drool on the controls.

Tomalon ached from head to foot—pain contemporary analgesics could not dispel. It was the ache of a phantom limb, of a severed arm, though Tomalon possessed all his bodily parts, and more. Tramping through the cathedral spaces of the ship he supposed that anyone seeing him would wonder at this strange apparition who seemed to be suffering some strange disease cloaking areas of his skin with glassy scabs, but his skin was his interface, and the phantom limb he sought, the ship itself.

An ECS pilot and weapons specialist as well as a student of AI/human synergy (his grand thesis concerned the direct interface between Iversus Skaidon and the Craystein AI, though not the first and certainly not the most definitive), he stood high on the list of applicants for this post. The fact that he was also a student of history swung it, for he learnt its lessons well. Many people, he knew, hated AI rulers of humanity. Others loved them and some worshipped them. He admired and, he felt, understood them. Considering his knowledge of that time before The Quiet War—when the AIs took over—he saw the lot of humanity much improved now. So now, he came to replace Varence and as closely link to an AI as presently possible without having his brain blown like a faulty fuse.

The huge interior of the ship consisted of movable sections. Weapons platforms and sensor arrays could be presented at the hull and later recalled inside to be repaired by interior autofactories. Living quarters could be shifted to safer areas within, or even ejected should the ship suffer an attack likely to destroy it. The bridge pod could be moved about inside to forever keep its location opaque to enemy scanning, and could similarly be ejected. Tomalon wondered if its present location, so far from his entry point, was a deliberate ploy on Occam's part so the AI could watch him for a little while before they finally sealed their interface, partial and impermanent though it might be.

Finally Tomalon reached the drop-shaft that would take him up to where the bridge pod presently extended, like the head of a giant, golden thistle from the ship's hull. He stepped into the irised gravity field, and as it drew him up he felt no reservations, no second thoughts. It seemed as if he had been preparing for this all his life. Departing the head of the drop-shaft he traversed a corridor he recognised as the one running through the stem to the pod itself. Clinging to the ceiling, a couple of crab maintenance drones observed him and he raised a hand in salute, before finally entering the pod.

Through the chainglass roof the nearby shipyard lay just visible, though the intense activity around it was not. Tomalon turned his attention to the rest of the pod.

Translucent consoles seemingly packed with fairy lights walled this place. Fixed to columns sunk into the black glass floor, in which the spill of optics flickered like synapses, an arc of command chairs faced the chainglass windows in the nose. The prime command chair, which looked more like a throne, lay at the centre of these. Why the other chairs remained here, Tomalon could not guess—the ship and its captain had required no command crew for more than fifty years. In reality the ship only needed a human captain to provide executive permission to its AI, and in fact not even that. Tomalon found himself in the strange position of having to relay Occam's orders to itself—a way of circumventing the old hard-wiring the ship contained.

"Occam," he asked out loud, and was unsurprised to receive no reply. The AI had always honed down its communications to the barest minimum during previous exchanges. Tomalon wondered if it missed Varence who, no longer supported by this ship's systems and that prosthetic being the intelligence of the AI itself, had quietly slid into death. He nodded to himself, stepped over to the command chair, and after a moment kicked off his slippers then shrugged off his coverall and tossed it on a nearby chair. Naked he seated himself, his forearms resting lightly on the chair arms and feet correctly positioned on the footrest. Immediately, with eerie silence, the interface connections swung out from underneath and behind the throne, and trailing skeins of optic cable closed in on him like an electric hand. The first connections were of the vambraces on both his arms—U-engine, fusion and thruster controls, then others began to mate all over his body. In those first moments he felt as if he were draining away as his consciousness expanded to encompass the ship, and the vast input from its sensors. He began to panic.

"Note the shipyard," Occam told him, "see how it grows."

The words brought immediate calm. He focused, and felt his nictitating membranes close down over his eyes and knew that to anyone observing they now looked blind white. But now he saw so much more. The shipyard was growing visibly amidst the swarm of constructor robots and telefactors: scaffolds webbing out into space and hull metal rapidly filling in behind.

"How big is it going to be?"

"Big enough. But what does its present designation tell you?"

Tomalon tried to remember, then found himself pulling the information as if from the aug he no longer wore, taking it from the very mind of Occam. "It does not yet have a name. Its designation is merely Shipyard 001 … ah, I see. We may be building hundreds of these?"

"So it would seem. This will be no small war."

Now Tomalon could look within the ship...himself. He enjoyed access to every internal cam and could gaze through the eyes of every drone or robot. Diagnostic systems came online, and he checked the readiness of the U-space engines, the fusion engines, the multitude of steering thrusters. Information flowed through him and not one detail bypassed him. He felt like a god.

"So, history student, what is the lesson we AIs have learned?"

Confusion, but only for a moment, for his close link to the mind of Occam enabled him to understand the AI's drift. "I can quote direct from a lecture I once heard: 'After the eighteenth century neither bravery nor moral superiority won wars, but factories and production.' That concerned the World War II and America's intervention, though it is equally as applicable now."

"Quite," Occam replied. "Do you feel ready to take this product into the fray?"

"I do," Tomalon replied, but he felt a moment of disquiet. His mind seemed to be operating with crystal clarity now and he saw many other historical parallels.

"But you feel some disquiet, I sense?"

"The story of the *Hood* and the *Bismarck* occurs to me."

"Ah, I see: The *Hood* was the largest and most powerful ship available to Britain at the start of World War II, but Hitler's *Bismarck* quickly destroyed it. Perhaps now would be a good time for you to check the weapons manifests and acquaint yourself with the armament we carry."

Tomalon's perception opened into and upon enormous weapons carousels, rail-guns, beam weapons, a cornucopia of death and destruction. He saw that included in this cornucopia were the new CTDs—contra-terrene devices—and realised that, being a god, here were his thunderbolts.

3.

They dined on mince, and slices of quince—

The Trajeen cargo runcible briefly came into view through the shuttle windows: five horn-shaped objects with tips overlapping bases in a curvilinear pentagon. Each of these objects was three hundred metres long with accommodation and R&D units clinging around its outer curve like the cells of a beehive. Tube walkways linked these conglomerations, and many solar panels glimmered like obsidian leaves. An orthogonal nest of plaited nanotube scaffolding poles enclosed the whole. Moria glimpsed the robots, one-man constructor pods and telefactors in the process of dismantling that scaffold. The glare of welders and cutting gear lit stars throughout the complex and plumes of water vapour swirled out like just-forming question marks over vacuum.

The shuttle swung in, taking the runcible out of view for a few minutes. Shadows then fell across the vessel and Moria saw some of those hexagonal units up close as the craft came in to dock. It shuddered into place, docking clamps engaged with a hollow clattering, followed by the whoosh of air filling a docking tunnel. After a moment, the disembarkation light came on and all the passengers began unstrapping themselves and pushing off from their seats to grab the safety rails leading to the airlock. Inside the shuttle it was nil gee, as in the tunnel leading to the complex.

"Best of luck," said Carolan as they reached the complex itself, then she slapped Moria on the shoulder and moved swiftly away. Moria guessed the woman's haste was instigated by the sight of the ECS officer heading this way across the embarkation area. She had only told Carolan that the AI contacted her concerning her Sylac aug and wanted to speak to her further, not daring to relate the circumstances of that contact. She pushed herself from the docking tube and settled down to the floor as the grav-plates within began to take hold.

"Moria Salem?" asked the man, smiling at her nicely.

"You know I am," she replied.

"Let's not be unpleasant about this," he told her, his smile becoming fixed.

Moria eyed him, realising he came suitably equipped to handle "unpleasantness." His shaven pate gleamed a head and shoulders above her and he probably massed about twice as much—none of that weight being fat. He was either a heavy-worlder or a man substantially boosted: bones and joints reinforced to withstand an implausible muscle mass.

"Where do I go?" Moria asked.

"With me of course." The man's smile lit again and it almost seemed genuine. Despite herself, Moria began warming to him.

He led her across the embarkation area to a nil-gee drop-shaft along which they towed themselves to a corridor. They traversed further shafts and corridors until reaching one of the tubes crossing vacuum between units of the complex. Moria now realised they were leaving the area in which she normally worked. Through the transparent tube wall she could see stars glimmering all around the swirled marble of Trajeen, and nearby lay a vertiginous view of the cargo runcible and surrounding facilities. A distant speck revealed itself as someone in a spacesuit, striding on gecko boots around a metallic curve, flipping a cable along behind. This gave scale to the view—an impressive though familiar sight to her.

The tunnel terminated at a coded security door. The man pressed his hand against a gene and palm reader of the kind that also ascertained that the hand's owner still lived—certain macabre scenarios briefly flitted through Moria's mind—then he input a code on a touch-plate.

"What's your name?" she asked.

He glanced at her. "George." An old and strangely prosaic name in this setting.

Beyond the door lay a whole unit Moria knew to be infrequently visited by the usual project crew. Rumour had it that its armour lay a metre thick and that it contained weapons arrays and its own independent drive. Grav dragged them to the floor within the inner lock, and while George opened the second door, Moria glanced up at the scanning drone suspended from the ceiling—suspiciously large power cables plumbed into it.

Inside, the carpeted corridor absorbed sound, and muted lighting from ornate light fitments lay easy on the eye. The carpet itself was decorated with repeating representations of the Trajeen AI and computer network. AIs were represented as red triangles, subminds were minor orange triangles, with variously coloured dots indicating servers and computers, and the whole being tangled in a three-dee web of com channels. The walls were clad with pillow-shaped foamstone blocks. Not so much bustle here—an oddly quiet and comfortable niche for something requiring no comfort. George led her to wooden panel doors and opened them onto a wide lounge alongside which long windows gave a panoramic view across the runcible.

"Please, take a seat." George gestured to a sofa.

Moria perched on the edge of one plush black fabric-covered sofa and surveyed the lounge. It seemed likely to her that much of this room's contents were either antique or indistinguishable reproduction. The oval table lying between the two sofas appeared to be made of genuine Earth-import wood, or maybe the table itself had been imported. Along one wall, on a worktop of polished stone, stood a collection of computers extending from the earliest PCs to present day. Behind them the racked wall contained a huge collection of ancient storage media: tapes, discs of many different sizes and formats, stacks of silicon data storage units, digital paper, carbon rod and early crystal, and much else she could not identify. In one corner squatted an insectile telefactor with forelimbs folded across its body as if it were in prayer; behind it lay the atmosphere-sealed shelves of a carousel packed with books. She realised the computers were all wired in and, by wear in the carpet below, that the telefactor frequently used them. It seemed the AI enjoyed access to much ancient information, though to what purpose she could not guess. A hobby? Historical research?

"A drink?"

Moria turned to see George standing by a drinks cabinet.

"Do you have greenwine?"

"Certainly."

He found a bottle Moria knew to be a rare vintage, and poured two glasses before coming over. He placed the drinks on the table and seated himself on the sofa opposite.

"So when does the AI talk to me?" She took a sip of her drink—ice cold in a crystal goblet lightly dusted with frost.

"It is talking to you now," George replied.

A beat.

"You're a Golem?"

"No, I am physically human but mentally a submind of the Trajeen System Cargo Runcible AI." He gestured towards his chest. "This body was grown in a vat, the mind programmed as an adjunct to myself."

Moria had not known this to be possible. It might not be, for AIs did not necessarily tell the truth.

"Okay." She took another drink to hide her confusion, then decided to play along with this. "Other than the fact that the aug I'm wearing might be something other than standard, I've something else bothering me."

George waited.

She continued: "Why did Sylac use his own name if he is a fugitive?"

"He conducted many operations in his surgery in Copranus City, working under the pseudonym Doctor Runciman Hyde." George winced. "A rather telling pseudonym... Only with you did he use his correct name. He is arrogant and wants us to know about his work. By using his true name, prior to closing his surgery and moving on, he knew we would eventually find out, and track down all those upon whom he conducted nonstandard augmentation."

"He has gone then?"

"We are searching for him at present, but he had two weeks in which to make his escape. Precisely at the time you experienced the enhanced level of aug function aboard the shuttle, over a hundred others experienced the same. However, only through you did we identify him."

"So what now?"

"Now I must make an assessment of you, your aug, and the synergetic combination you represent." George leaned forwards and now Moria noticed something weird about his eyes: the irises seemed to have become evenly spoked and metallic. "I will make an optic linkage to your aug, and in a virtuality of your choosing, we will explore your potential or...otherwise."

"I suppose that virtuality is the only choice I have in this matter?"

"Precisely."

"I think we interrupted their dinner break," said Jean, adding, "It seems they like to play with their food."

Alan Grace, a tough and experienced ECS monitor, pulled himself down beside a laser drill rig and vomited. With no gravity to drag it down the vomit shot with amazing speed across ten metres of air space to splash on a wall. The other two ECS monitors were further back in the factory, short ropes securing them to the floor and one of them tightening a tourniquet just above the other's right knee. Below that knee remained nothing but shreds. The woman felt no pain though, the drug patch on her neck having sent her to glittering fairyland.

"Urbanus, find the grav-plate controls and see if you can route in power—slowly," Jebel instructed, keeping his tone succinct, factual.

Droplets of blood and other fluids swirled across the nightmare scene like plastic beads. There were three corpses here. The Prador had secured them to the wall with some sort of resin. The left-hand one, a man, had suffered most. His arms were gone below the elbows and what remained of his guts hung out. It seemed evident, by the ties above his elbows—little different from the tourniquet presently being applied to the wounded monitor—and by the tubes plumbed into his carotids leading to some kind of pressure bag, that the aliens had kept him alive while they took him apart. His arms were nowhere in the vicinity. It seemed obvious what the Prador had done with the parts they removed. The other two corpses were headless. One head spun slowly a few metres below the ceiling, whilst the other lodged amid some nearby pipework. Jebel guessed the Prador killed their prisoners upon sighting him and the others. He glanced down at his right hand and saw it quivering. Mentally he ticked things off: hostile, horrible-looking bastards, eat people, torture people. Redeeming characteristics: none found. He felt a mad giggle rising in his chest and stamped on it hard.

Turning away, Jebel closed his eyes and tried to distance himself from what he felt. But one fact kept replaying in his mind: these people were almost certainly civilians, so being a noncombatant just did not help. Cirrella's apartment lay a few floors down from here and some way ahead. He considered just leaving the others and going his own way, going to find out, but self-discipline and training won out in the end. By remaining part of the overall strategy to retake this part of the station he stood a better chance of helping her, and others like her. If he went off on his own he would probably end up dead. Simple really, but not something he could accept on an emotional level.

"I've rerouted connections," said Urbanus over comlink, "and *Avalon* is supplying power. The machinery will remain offline but I am beginning to power-up the grav-plates now."

Slowly, gravity returned. Throughout the factory, objects began settling to the floor. Jebel watched the beads drop and the corpses sag. He glanced back as other similarly insalubrious objects pattered down. His own feet shortly touched a floor becoming slick with blood.

"That's better," said Alan Grace, holding his gut.

Urbanus returned. "*Avalon* is sending others to secure this area." The Golem nodded to the wounded monitor. "They'll take her back to the nearest med bay."

Within minutes the backup team arrived, and medics

tended the wounded monitor while others began to reconnect shattered optic junctions to pincams. Com became clearer and for a second or two Jebel found his aug function trying to reinstate. Via com, the station AI informed him, "You are now in command, Jebel Krong, ranking increased by two points. Continue your mission, which is to get out as many civilians as possible, but understand your time is now limited. We have confirmation that the Prador are returning to their shuttle. Once that shuttle departs, this station is likely to become the prime target of the mother ship."

Please let Cirrella be safe now...

"What about the ECS ships?"

"All destroyed."

It struck him in the guts. They won nothing here—they were just trying to limit their losses. His aug then fully reinstated long enough for him to receive details of the areas he must now sweep, but still no message from Cirrella. He decided that the moment they were recalled he would set out by himself and find her, but other things needed doing now.

"Very well." Jebel scanned his command. "We continue. I for one want to kill some more of these fuckers."

His team growled assent.

He led his comrades from the factory into further nil-gee areas, finally reaching the designated meeting point—a spherical chamber at the junction of numerous corridors in the centre of which stood a cypress tree, its limbs shattered. There he gave instructions to the other units, and they moved on.

"If they're retreating to their ship, we'll probably not run into any more ambushes," Jean observed.

"Okay, let's pick up the pace."

They moved faster for another quarter of an hour before Urbanus abruptly called, "Halt!"

Jebel glared at the Golem, but Urbanus, as coolly as his name, directed Jebel's attention to certain small cylindrical objects affixed to the ceiling ahead. "I don't know what they are, but they're certainly not ours."

"Shoot one of them," Jebel instructed.

In one smooth movement Urbanus raised and fired his carbine. The cylinders detonated in multiple blasts, filling the corridor ahead with fire and shrapnel.

"Bastards," Jebel commented, and slowed the pace again.

However, by Jebel's estimation they had penetrated halfway into the area held by the Prador. Finally they worked their way up to a long shopping mall with balconies overlooking a park extending through a kilometre-long tube. And once again sighted the enemy.

George—she could no longer think of the AI as a submind of the "Trajeen System Cargo Runcible AI"—was a presence at her shoulder while she demonstrated the trail of logic leading her to the truth about the crashed shuttles. Occasionally she surfaced from the virtuality to glance aside at the optic cable snaking down over her shoulder from the aug, and sometimes to take a sip of wine from her glass which, by some hidden mechanism, remained chilled all this while.

"U-space calculations again, and runcible mechanics," George instructed.

Moria began by modelling the cargo gates at Trajeen and Boh in her aug and started to run the calculations involved in sending something through—the same calculations an AI needed to make, in nanoseconds, at each transmission. The Trajeen gate, relative to the one orbiting Boh, was travelling 70,000 kph faster. Simplified, the calculation involved the input of energy required to push the object through the

Skaidon warp plus the energy required to accelerate it to 70,000 km/h so that basically, when it came out of the gate at the other end, it neither accelerated nor decelerated. But that was an extreme simplification. Between the gates, in U-space, Einsteinian rules ceased to apply while the object accelerated to a speed beyond C, relative to realspace, though in U-space where such measures did not apply it moved not at all and no time passed ... didn't really exist. Moria didn't go there, that being the territory of the AIs. She concentrated on the simpler calculations, for though the broad difference between the two gates was a speed of 70,000 kph, obtaining the exact figure involved factoring in angular momentums and solving rather esoteric force vectors. Another factor in the calculation was the C energy, this being the input energy of the transmission and the energy drawn into the runcible buffers at the destination runcible. The first transmission ever conducted had been unbuffered. A pea was sent, in deference to Iversus Skaidon's obsession with the poem "The Owl and the Pussycat" by Edward Lear—a beautiful pea-green boat, though later "pea-green" being assigned to a particle tentatively identified as a tachyon. Other terms were also later assigned: travellers became quince and the gates became runcibles. The pea came out of the receiving end where the Einsteinian universe ruthlessly reapplied its rules. It exited at a fraction below light speed and caused an explosion that vaporized most of the surrounding base, killing numerous researchers. Luckily, Moria felt, they decided not to make the test using an owl or a pussycat... or a boat. She solved the vectors, quickly and efficiently.

"Impressive," said George, "though still the product of linear thinking."

"A fact of which every human runcible technician is aware," Moria replied dryly.

Humans who worked on runcibles were endlessly frustrated

by this science which lay completely at a tangent to human linear thinking. Yes, a human could comprehend sections of the mathematics and complex technology of everything outside the Skaidon warp, and with augmentation a single human might one day be able to encompass it all. But past the warp you stepped beyond an event horizon not dissimilar to that of a black hole. The rules broke down, things started to make no sense to a product of biological evolution. Every object transmitted through a runcible came with its own information package detailing its energy vectors, vectors which also involved time. In U-space all Skaidon warps are in the same place at the same time which is no-time, in no-space. The object doesn't cease to exist for there is no time for it to do so. How do the AIs controlling the receiving runcibles know when to pull the object out? By reading the information package. Essentially everything ever transmitted or to be transmitted exists in U-space... where nothing exists but does... It gave Moria a headache just to try to encompass the twisted logic without getting involved in the mathematics and technology involved in what was called "the spoon." That headache became worse when she contemplated such things as time-inconsistent runcibles and the possibility of receiving something before it was ever transmitted.

"Let me see. You have been involved in the design and construction of warp adjustment generators?"

"Yes, but I was beginning to lose grip on the mathematics."

"Well, as I suspected, you have achieved synergy with your augmentation—you are more closely interfaced than anyone before now."

Remembering what happened to Iversus Skaidon and knowing the dangers of direct interfacing with AI, she asked, "Is this going to kill me?"

"Your augmentation is not an artificial intelligence. It is a computer, a glorified modem, a junction box. I understand your fears but they are not relevant here. The synergy achieved by direct interfacing a human mind with AI causes a kind of feedback loop sending both minds into a cyclic critical escalation, which results in the less sturdy mind being overloaded … usually the human."

"Usually the human?"

"There are sparsely documented cases of the reverse happening, though no real confirmation, but we are digressing here. It seems Aubron Sylac has truly achieved something of note here. When you return from your next break, I am going to move you into the Control Centre where you will join those overseeing the first test. Some training will be required, but I trust you will be adequately able."

"That's it?" Moria returned to full-on reality.

George leant forwards. "That is it, for now."

Down below Jebel that multi-legged, multi-murderer Vortex crouched, like a nightmare gatekeeper to Hell, atop the statue of some premillennial astronaut, its attention focused on the scene below. The smaller Prador were scuttling along at ground level through the long tubular park, digging their sharp feet into the ground and scuffing up turf to keep from going airborne as they towed along lines of prisoners all linked together. So, taking slaves or stocking their larder? Which is it? Both? Only a quarter of an hour before, Jebel raised to his eyes the monocular Jean passed him and noted with angry horror that the prisoners were not tied to each other, but stapled hand to hand. Listening, he could just hear the yelling and cacophony which also seemed the product of some lower circle of the pit. He scanned faces—yelling, terrified, some unconscious. It was not by her face that he identified her, but by the blonde hair in a plait and the jeans and green blouse. Something really snapped inside him then, but he tried to control his visible reaction.

"Okay," he turned to his comrades, noting the slightly wary look they were giving him. "We've got Vortex and ten of his little bastards down there." He turned on his comlink and in brief conversations with the other unit leaders ascertained their positions and gave them their instructions. The ECS grunts were closer to the Prador, and down towards Jebel's right. His throat dry, he continued, "If this goes wrong you are to hit those ten little shits and grab as many of those prisoners as you can. Choose your targets carefully, those are Polity citizens down there." What else could he say? If his plan worked there should be no shooting. Now he returned his attention to his own people. "Who has the gecko mines?" he asked.

Jean unslung her pack and opened it. Jebel took out the square case inside and popped it open. Twelve mines rested inside, each a small ovoid that could sit in the palm of a hand. They were programmable and could be set to detonate in many different ways. The gecko pads, presently covered by nilfrict paper, would stick to just about anything. He selected five mines and set them for detonation should any attempt be made to remove them, also to be detonated by the remote transmitter, which he took from the box and placed in his pocket. Just as a precaution he also set them to a timed detonation of one hour. He placed the mines in pockets on his utility belt.

"You," he stabbed a finger at Urbanus, "will come over the top of the park with me. I want you positioned, along with three others, over on those balconies." Jebel pointed to some jutting balconies trailing red clematis over on the far side, directly adjacent to Vortex. "And you, Jean, will take the others and find a similar position on this side. There are probably balconies further along here."

"Yourself?" Urbanus asked.

"We know what will happen. If we attack, they'll just kill indiscriminately. We attack as a last resort. This Vortex is obviously the big shot around here and perhaps places some importance upon his own survival. I am going to come down on him from above—up close and personal."

"I see," said Urbanus doubtfully. "And your chances of surviving?"

"Well, that's up to all of you, when you cover my escape."

Now, crouched upside down between lighting units above the monstrous Prador, Jebel Krong gazed down at the hellish scene trying again to pick out Cirrella. He could not see her, and wondered if he had really seen her at all. But then the screams and bellows from below impinged once again and the ball of rage growing inside him expanded. He changed his com frequency to that which the Prador were using. Jebel was able to learn nothing as the creatures communicated with some kind of esoteric code. But the possibility that Vortex would hear what he needed to say and be able to understand it was his only one option here. Jebel straightened his legs hard and hurtled headfirst down towards the Prador.

What the fuck am I doing?

At the last moment Jebel flipped his body, came down on the Prador feet first, absorbing the impact with his legs and slapping down the two gecko mines he held. They stuck hard and he managed to stop himself from flying away again by holding onto them.

"Okay, fuck-head. I just stuck two mines on you." Steadied now, Jebel pulled the other mines from his belt and slapped them down. Vortex froze in position, obviously surprised—perhaps the creature had not expected a human to dare coming this close. "Oh look, three more. I hope you've got your translator on, because if we don't talk about this, you are crab paste."

One claw suddenly snapped up past the Prador's visual turret. Jebel sprang away as it slammed close to where he had crouched.

"Now!" over com.

Missiles streaked in from either side, exploding the statue underneath Vortex. As Jebel hurtled back up towards the ceiling he saw the creature swivelling back and raising one of those Gatling rail-guns towards him, but the missile blasts sent Vortex tumbling through the air. A line of rail-gun missiles tracked across the ceiling, putting out lights and filling the air with glittering fragments. Jebel reached a gap between lighting units and quickly pulled himself to cover, bouncing through the frameworks and shadow. Vortex fired again, but Jebel realised the Prador wasn't shooting at any target, but using the gun's recoil to drive itself down to the branches of an apple tree where it clung on.

"Do you hear me, Vortex?"

The other Prador were shooting at the balconies. Pieces of stonework and clematis flowers rained down. After a moment this firing ceased.

"I hear you," came the reply.

"Did you hear what I just said to you while I stuck those mines on your back?"

"I heard."

"Well this is the deal. You release those prisoners and I'll shut down those mines, at which point they'll auto detach." It was a lie—Jebel did not intend removing the mines.

Some instruction, some signal, maybe just the twitch of a claw. Suddenly the smaller Prador turned on their captives and were firing. Pieces of human bodies were flying in every direction, and with no gravity here they just kept on spreading—an ever-growing gory explosion.

No deal.

Cirrella.

Jebel activated the mines and watched the explosion blow away Vortex's main body, but leave the creature's legs hanging in the apple tree. He then took up his missile launcher and hurled himself down towards the mayhem, firing on the other creatures from midair, blasting carapace and armoured limbs in every direction. He was not thinking anymore—didn't care. Coming down in the branches of the tree in which Vortex's limbs still hung, he pulled himself down and tried to stay on the ground. The grass was spattered with green liquid and pieces of carapace, and similar material drifted through the air all about him. He was breathing Prador blood. He saw a man tumbling past, wrapped in his own intestines. Projectiles were slamming into everything around Jebel, but just seemed to miss him every time. Crawling, he pulled himself along, grabbing handholds on bloody grass and through an equally gory rose bed. Only here the blood was red. One of the smaller Prador rose bubbling beside him, then exploded, spattering him with strong-smelling flesh. Choking, he crawled on—he did not know for how long and only realised time had passed as the intensity of fire from all sides finally reduced. He gazed around at mayhem partially concealed by a gory haze and could see no Prador standing, few humans too. At some point grav came back on, but he continued to crawl. How he found her he did not know. He sat stroking her hair, eyes averted from where her leg and half her torso had been torn away

"We have to get away, now." Urbanus, leaning over him.

Cirrella behind him and somehow a weapon back in his hands. More Prador coming.

Urbanus again. "I can't let you do this."

The blow to Jebel's temple brought welcome oblivion.

In his frustration Captain Immanence snatched up a second-child in his remaining claw and held it squealing above the deck. The other two quickly fled through the open door into the sanctum, but the fascination of "it's not me this time" held them there while Immanence smashed their brother repeatedly against the wall, before dropping the quivering wreckage.

These humans thought to try and make deals?

Immanence bubbled with rage.

"One of you come here and feed this to me, the other one go and fetch Vagule," he grated out in the sawing crunching Prador language.

The two second-children at once began to squabble. Neither of them wanted the chore of feeding their brother to Immanence while he was in this mood.

"Now!"

One second-child possessed the presence of mind to dash away leaving the other one quivering in the doorway. Immanence made a note to himself to remember that—the runner might possess the characteristics to survive into first-childhood. The remaining second-child came over, still quivering and now making an obeisant whining. It picked up a hunk of carapace with flesh and purple-green organs still clinging inside and held it up to the captain. Immanence took it with his mandibles and chewed contemplatively. Eating always calmed him, and he was in a slightly better frame of mind—for a Prador—when Vagule, one of his two remaining first-children, arrived.

Immanence studied Vagule. The first-child had yet to attain the bulk of Vortex and there was a healing crack in its carapace, no doubt made by that other now-dead first-child. Sucking the flesh from a small claw, Immanence began to see the plus side of things. Vortex, having attained full growth, had only been maintained in permanent adolescence by the pheromones the old adult emitted and by certain additives to his food. Inevitably some mission would have taken him away from that diet and those pheromones long enough for him to make the transition into full adulthood and thus become a competitor. Then it would have been necessary to dispense with him. Vagule, however, lay some time away from that stage in his life where the dietary changes became necessary.

"You are now the Prime," Immanence told Vagule. "Assign your current projects to Gnores and stand ready to deal with the human prisoners. You may move into Vortex's cell. I will provide the code keys to all his research and stored files."

"What happened to Vortex?" Vagule asked.

"He became careless and humans killed him. You may study the recorded data I will send over to Vortex's cell and thereby learn from his mistake. Now leave."

Vagule spun round and moved away fast, no doubt anxious to sample the privileges of his new position. Immanence dismissed the remaining second-child—the other one did not return—and closed the sanctum doors behind it. After a moment he caused his chouds to call up views of the station, and status reports on the ship's systems. Everything seemed functional, and all he required now was for the shuttle to get out of the way. He checked the status of that operation and ascertained that all but a few of the second-children were aboard. He also discovered that one large second-child had begun issuing orders and dealing out shell-cracks to those who did not obey with sufficient alacrity—another first-child candidate.

Immanence opened com to that individual. "You, XF-326, are now in command. Close up the shuttle and depart the station."

"The others?"

"Are dragging their belly plates. There are two kinds of Prador, XF-326, the quick and the dead. Decide now which you want to be."

Sudden frenetic activity ensued within the shuttle. The doors began to close. One last second-child made it inside the shuttle, trying to drag after it a chain of prisoners. It managed to get three and a half of the humans through. After another few minutes, Immanence observed explosions as the Prador blew docking clamps the station AI had previously locked. The shuttle departed, ripping pieces of the station away and snapping the boarding tube like a stretched worm. Small, struggling and expiring objects followed it into vacuum, some of them were second-children, most were dancing chains of stapled-together humans.

"Now we will see about deals," said Immanence.

He scanned the station along its entire length. Large heat sources were evident around those Polity matter transmission devices, which probably meant humans were crowding there. He ran some calculations and came up with a rough estimate: about four thousand humans still remained aboard, though this number was dropping at an alarming rate. Immanence realised they must be throwing them through the matter transmitters at a phenomenal rate. He was planning to wait until the shuttle returned to its bay aboard his ship, but if he did that his kill number might well drop by two-thirds.

Weapons online.

Something stung Jebel's neck and coming to a half-conscious state he fought to return to oblivion. It was like waking to the sure knowledge of an imminent bad hangover, though infinitely worse. He knew things were going to hurt him. Badly. But as consciousness finally did return the expected pain did not rush in, and he only felt numb inside. On his outside, however, cuts and bruises impinged and his head ached as if someone ran a potato peeler around inside his skull.

"I won't ask if you're okay," said Urbanus.

Lying on the floor, with something tucked underneath his head and a yelling crowd all around him, Jebel stared at the Golem squatting beside him. Without Urbanus' intervention he would not have had to wake to this. He tried to find some anger at that, but it eluded him.

"What happened?"

Urbanus nodded over nearby, so Jebel hauled himself up a little to look. They were in a runcible embarkation lounge surrounded by crowds of people packed in tight: families with children, pets, hastily gathered belongings. Nearby were rows of the injured, prostrate like him but being tended by medical personnel and a couple of mobile autodocs, like chrome beetles.

"We managed to get twenty of them out," Urbanus told him.

Jebel winced, but it seemed almost an automatic reaction.

"Why did you stop me?" he asked.

"Because you were intent on killing yourself."

"Last I heard, laws against suicide were pulled a few centuries ago."

"Then I stopped you for selfish purposes and for the Polity. I did not want you to die, and one such as yourself will be useful in what is to come."

Jebel again tried to feel some anger at the Golem, but the anger now eating away his internal numbness focused in only one direction, and Urbanus possessed too few limbs to be a candidate.

"If you wish, I can return your weapon and you can go kill

some more of them. You'll die. Either by them killing you or when this station is destroyed as seems sure to happen."

Jebel hauled himself up further until sitting upright. Waves of dizziness blurred his surroundings, and now he smelt burning and heard the distant sounds of weapons fire. "Where are we?"

"Within the area the Prador cut off. We couldn't get out, and now our best chance of escaping lies through this runcible." Urbanus pointed.

Jebel stood and gazed over the heads of the crowd. ECS commandos and station personnel ringed the runcible, the two bull-horns of its gateposts mounted on a black glass dais. Through a gap in this cordon a line of people four across was filing up to the Skaidon warp and stepping through, as through the skin of a bubble, and disappearing. Despite the racket of the surrounding crowd, it all seemed pretty orderly. He guessed that would soon change if the Prador entered this place.

"Why aren't the Prador here?" he asked. "You told me a while ago that they might try to seize this runcible."

"Two reasons, I suspect. They are withdrawing from the station, probably because something is imminent from the mother ship. They are also probably aware that if they got close to the runcible, *Avalon* would destroy it, taking many of them with it."

Jebel absorbed that. Though Urbanus had previously explained that the station AI might be prepared to destroy the runcible rather than allow these Prador to get their claws on it, he had not thought to ask why it was so important. You needed AIs to operate runcibles and AIs the Prador did not possess.

"That would kill all these people as well. Why? What use would a runcible be to the Prador?"

"Despite all the claims to the contrary, we haven't really

fathomed how advanced these creatures are. Runcible technology, even without AI control, could be used as a powerful weapon. And from recent experience it seems likely that would be just how they would use it."

Jebel nodded. "Is it open port now?" He glanced over at those filing through the Skaidon warp.

"For the civilians, at present. But it won't be for us when our slot comes up in about five minutes."

"Why not?"

"Because we are needed," said Urbanus. "Do you think for one moment that only *Avalon Station* is under attack?"

Immanence first launched a small swarm of missiles carrying simple chemical-explosive warheads, and watched with every sensor at his disposal. The swarm, first accelerated by rail-gun, ignited solid-fuel rockets to disperse and then bring the missiles in to target points all along the station. Within fifty kilometres of the station they began to detonate as defence lasers and masers fired. Immanence ran tactical programs to log the positions of those defences and then accelerated his ship towards the station. Missiles were now rising up from the defence positions, preceded by a storm of solid rail-gun projectiles. The captain supposed the AI was firing every weapon it controlled. What else could it do?

A thousand kilometres out he picked his targets. Five hundred kilometres out the rail-gun missiles began to impact on his ship's hull. Again, piezoelectric layers and thermal generators stacked up the charge inside his vessel and he released it through all four particle cannons. The beams bored into the station's hull, air and fire exploding out behind as they cut trenches to their targets. Some of those defence positions just disappeared, others blew glowing craters as stored munitions detonated. Immanence veered his ship, passing over the station. More firing from down there, and in return, stabs from the particle beams taking out their sources. He swept in a long, slow turn, and approached again. This time he selected four particular warheads: stasis-contained antimatter wrapped in a layer of hydrogen compressed to a metallic state. He veered again, firing, and watched these lethal devices speed down towards the station as he accelerated away. Still some defences, for one of the missiles was struck and bloomed into an expanding sphere of fire, bright as a sun. This sphere touched off a second missile which created a similar explosion nearer to the station, but ahead of this one's blast wave, the two others struck.

Two explosions ate through the Polity station in seeming slow motion. Hull metal peeled up before the blast waves and ablated away. White-hot structural beams hurtled out, losing their shape as they turned to liquid then gas. The station burned and broke apart, its debris melting away as the two explosions melded into one. The sleet of radiation struck Immanence's ship, soaking into screening and causing various detectors to scream their alarms. But before the main blast front reached it, he dropped his ship into U-space, clattering his mandibles in delight all the while.

4.

They sailed away, for a year and a day–

Moria sipped her greenwine—an inferior quality to the one George provided—and gazed across the city bar. There were many more uniforms visible now: the plain green or khaki of ECS soldiers on leave, and occasionally those wearing chameleon-cloth fatigues underneath thin, white coveralls worn to make those soldiers visible, but easily torn away. These latter troops were always armed, always sharp-eyed and never drank. Auging in to the newsnets Moria had learned about a missile being fired at a military AGC and a bomb exploding in a bar like this one. She had seen a four-man team of soldiers—two of them Golem—marching away at gunpoint someone in civilian dress. Separatists. They were always present on Trajeen, and soon captured or killed the moment they acted, but now it seemed they had become more active.

"This place is doing a good trade," said Carolan. "The economic benefits of war."

"Well the troops need to be fed and watered, then you get the herd instinct operating for the civilians. They don't want to be alone when stuff like this is happening." Daven Xing glanced at Moria and winked.

Ellen—Carolan's companion—gazed at Daven over her beer as if he had just issued a wet fart. Moria couldn't decide if Ellen disliked him intensely, or the opposite and was trying hard to conceal it. At one time Moria would have been fascinated by the interplay and perhaps considered how best to defend her territory—just on principle since after being her lover for two weeks Daven no longer really interested her. But her last shift at the gate project changed her entire outlook. She possessed no patience for such games, or the interest in such petty concerns.

After another sip of wine, Moria considered her last three-month shift. She thought her first session with George might be her last, but he recalled her time and again, and after each session her job description changed. He kept promoting her, yet she no longer felt the same about that anymore as she explored the realms of her mind in conjunction with the Sylac aug. Some called her "aug happy" but it seemed so much more than that.

"I hear you've been wowing them in the Control Centre?" said Carolan. "In fact you've been the talk of the project for some time now." She glanced at Daven. "And that George has taken a very special interest in you."

"Who's this George?" asked Daven with mock jealousy.

Moria grinned at him. Yes, she was really no longer interested in him now. "George is the AI up there."

"But not just that," Carolan added sneakily. "He runs a submind in a tank-grown human body. A *male* human body."

"Ah, I see," said Daven.

Moria supposed it was time now for a little fencing—for her to defend her position. She could not be bothered. Shrugging, she said, "I never knew they could do that, nor that it is allowed." Seeing that Moria did not intend to take the bait, Carolan gave up on that line and the conversation turned to the moral implications of AIs using human bodies. Moria let it drift away from her and continued with her introspection. She had learnt more and encompassed more while working from the Control Centre, yet George, though no longer testing her and her aug, or promoting her, for there was no higher she could go, kept stopping by and increasing her workload, and she kept on managing to sustain each increase. A peevish annoyance at her presence was the first reaction from the others in the Centre, then growing respect and a kind of awe. Out of the eight individuals there, none was really in charge since they all worked a specific area of competence under George. However, Moria's area of competence just kept expanding and she realised that the others had come to defer to her. But obviously, elsewhere, gossip-mongers like Carolan were traducing her.

At the month end, George entered the Control Centre. "We are nearly ready now," he said. "We don't need the buffers at this end as the test will be a one-way transference to the Boh cargo runcible in two weeks' time." He looked around at them all. "You will monitor the automatics, gather data throughout the test at this end. I'll want the data built into logic trees in order of importance and with relevancy connections, even though they might be assigned outside the present field of study." He now turned to Moria. "The same is obviously required at the other end. When you return from your break, you and I are going to Boh."

And this was her break. Why did she now find it so difficult to involve herself at an utterly human level? Was she obsessing about her own self-importance? She felt not. Perhaps being so deeply connected into her aug and its functions she was simply becoming less human. She gazed at her companions, drained her glass, then stood, smiling tightly.

"I've some things I need to prepare before I head back, so I'm afraid I'll have to leave you now."

A predatory look passed from Ellen to Daven, and he

gave Moria a speculative look in return. Leave them to it. The imminent runcible test was so much more important … and interesting. Moria moved from the bar feeling her companions' eyes upon her, and knew she would once again become the subject of their conversation. Outside the bar she stood in the street. The road and pavements were slick with rain water and the slime trail left by a groundskate presently flopping its way along a few metres from her. She stared at the reflection of Vina in that trail, glanced at a group of soldiers climbing from a hydrocab—probably just in from the growing encampment just outside town—and decided that if she hurried she could catch a shuttle to the runcible within an hour. Upon her arrival there she did not suppose it would be long before she was aboard a ship to Boh. There seemed little more she wanted to involve herself in down here, and so much more up there.

Second-child GJ-26, though honoured by being given the name Skulker, had yet to see his feed changed by Harl so he too could make the transition to first-childhood. As he crouched in blue gloom below matted tendrils and saucer leaves holding mucous-locked water in their upper, bright red surfaces, he understood the reasons for this, but could not help but feel some resentment. He was a small second-child, and becoming adept at concealing himself in this jungle made him a perfect scout for Prador land forces—an advantage they needed against the smaller, chameleon-cloth-concealed humans.

Skulker reached up, snipped through the tendril mat and pulled down some of the dished leaves. Carefully he smeared their slimy contents all over his carapace, claws and legs. Settling himself down for a while, he periodically checked the tackiness of his coating as it dried. When it finally reached readiness he began to scoop up organic debris from the ground and flip them all over himself. Leaf litter and pieces of dead tendril stuck, small fungal spheroids lodged amidst all this. Turning his eye-palps to inspect himself he finally finished the camouflage job with sprinklings of the grey underlying soil. Now he was ready.

First-child Harl's instructions were for him to spy-out the disposition of Polity forces arrayed on the jungle slopes above, then personally return with the information to the Prador temporary headquarters here, since there was now a suspicion that the humans had cracked their com codes. As on previous occasions he must flee if seen and not engage with the enemy unless cornered. Such instructions did not sit well with preadolescent or adolescent Prador, since that required that they override their instinctive aggression. Skulker did not find obedience so difficult. Intellectualizing the whole affair, he managed to displace the satisfaction of individual kills with the slaughter of many humans in which his information resulted.

Moving carefully, for the natural camouflage glue needed to dry, Skulker moved off between the plaited stalks and scaly sprouts of this planet's vegetation. On his light weapons harness he carried only a translator, grenades and a small assassin-spec rail-gun—the weapons he hoped never to need. In his heart he carried a hatred of the soft-bodied alien enemy, the sure knowledge that they would be defeated, and that he would survive to become a first-child Prime. Other Prador died. It would not happen to him.

After a kilometre the ground began to slope upwards and white rocks stained here and there with blue sap began to poke through. Now listening intently and stopping to sample the occasional strange odour in the air, Skulker froze when a meaty scent wafted towards him and he heard sudden movement ahead. It was difficult to see for any distance now, since spiny epiphytes sprouted in balls from the stems, stalks and trunks ahead. Skulker drew his rail-gun and held a chlorine smoke grenade in one of his hands ready to cover his retreat. Advancing, precisely sliding his sharp feet into the ground so as not to rustle the leaf litter, he closed on the sound and the source of that smell like some arachnoid spectre. Then upon seeing it, finally allowed himself to relax.

The creature's white teardrop body terminated at the narrow end in a ring of tentacles around a red gullet. Its hind limbs were long—the spiked knees high above its bloated back end—its forelimbs short and braced out sideways with twin toes buried in the ground. Skulker encountered many of these and had even tried eating one. That experiment resulted in squirming blue worms in his every bowel movement until he took a course of acidifier pellets to strip out the inner layers of his gut. It was not an experience he intended to repeat. In itself the creature would have been of no further interest to him, but its meal was.

The human's head was missing, as was one of its arms, one of its legs and a large proportion of the torso into which the native creature now dipped its head. Skulker moved out of concealment, noisily, but the creature did not seem to notice. Skulker then prodded it with his rail-gun. Finally acknowledging his presence it raised its tentacled front end and with a burping squawk launched itself up through the canopy, then went crashing away above.

Moving close to the human remains, Skulker began searching them. He removed a bracelet from the remaining wrist and played with the controls for a moment until some pictures began to appear on a small screen. These were all of humans doing whatever it was that humans did. One of them might be of the individual here. Skulker would not have been able to tell even if this one retained its head. He placed the bracelet in one of the pockets of his weapons harness—maybe Prador Intelligence would find some use for it—and continued his search, but found nothing more of note. He was eyeing the chameleon-cloth of the remaining uniform, when a new smell reached his senses over the meat smell, then he heard the voices.

"She's over this way," said one.

"Seems a damned long way for her to be carried by the blast," said the other.

"Wasn't the blast that carried her—one of those boschens dragged her from the temporary morgue. They've been doing a lot of that lately."

Skulker looked round in confusion for the voices sounded as if they were coming from upslope, yet he could hear movement from downslope and also to his left. He began to move stealthily to his right, where luckily the ground lay soft and thick with decaying vegetation.

"I don't know why they do it when human flesh poisons them—shame it doesn't do the same to the Prador."

"Poison would be good, but a gecko mine is so much more satisfying."

"True, very true."

Now there seemed to be movement over to his right, and after a moment Skulker smelt burnt metal, heard the hum of a grav-motor and a loud crackling—almost certainly one of those human AG gun platforms settling through the canopy. What to do? He could throw grenades now and run, but those on the platform would pursue. He could probably escape, but with none of the information first-child Harl sent him to obtain. Using a technique almost instinctive on home-world for burying oneself in mud, Skulker quickly buried himself in leaf-litter and soft dirt, with only his eye-palps and the snout of his rail-gun above the surface.

"Did you hear that?"

"Probably a boschen heard us and made like a frog… ah,

here we are."

Skulker slowly turned his eye-palps. The two humans were behind him! How did they get there and what were those other sounds in the surrounding jungle? The gun platform sound seemed to have disappeared, and the smell of hot metal displaced by one of burning vegetation. Skulker decided to stay very still and do nothing until he assessed this situation, for he was very good at skulking.

"Not much left of her is there, Jebel?" said the female of the two.

"Lucky there's anything at all."

An ECS-issue enviroboot came down on Skulker's back, then the female stepped over him. The one addressed as "Jebel" stepped on him next, but halted and stood there with both his boots on Prador carapace. The tension inside Skulker grew to snapping point as the man leisurely surveyed his surroundings, then seemed to notice something at his feet.

"Oh dear," the man said.

"What's up?" asked the woman.

Skulker pressed one of his thin fingers into the priming pit of his grenade and slightly tightened the pressure on the trigger of his rail-gun. The man squatted down, his head only a metre from the second-child's eye-palps. He began to do something with his footwear.

"This damned ground isn't very good for enviroboots."

After a moment he finished his chore then stood and stepped from Skulker's back, clipping an eye-palp with his boot on the way. With one eye watery and blurred Skulker followed the man's progress over to the woman, who was unfolding a body bag beside the corpse. He should not have moved his eye-palps.

"Prador!" the woman bellowed, throwing herself to one side.

Skulker triggered his gun, but the man also hurled himself aside, acrobatically bouncing to concealment faster than Skulker could track. He heaved himself upright, showering litter, tossed the grenade. A stalk exploded beside him and another blast excavated a cavity in the ground before him. Flinging himself sideways, he tracked fire around, severing stalks and raining down foliage and tendrils. His grenade blew, spewing out poisonous smoke. Then he heard the whickering sound of a laser, a flash of brightness blinded him and sharp pain ensued. With his lower turret-eyes Skulker caught a horrifying glimpse of his two eye-palps dropping, smoking, to the ground. He turned and ran. More explosions all around him, more weapons fire cutting through the jungle, but now with no eye-palps he could no longer look behind him. Something singed his back end, cracking carapace.

"Over there! Get the bastard!"

Fire from a rail-gun cut down to his left from above and Skulker heard the drone of a gun platform. He shot to his right, turning sideways to fling himself through a gap in the jungle. Something whoomphed behind him and smoke and flame rolled above. Skulker ran just as fast as he could, bouncing from stems, falling occasionally, and coming close to obliteration far too often. The chase lasted an hour and only when the explosions and sounds of firing moved off ahead and to his right did he think he at last stood some chance of escape. The pursuit finally died away in the night, and knowing that without his eye-palps he could be nowhere near as effective as normal, he finally, reluctantly, returned to base.

"Report," said Harl, flicking his eye-palps once towards Skulker before returning his attention to a console he held in one large claw. Four other first-children stood nearby beside a Prador landing craft. With the eager assistance of numerous second-children, they were assembling a ground-effect particle cannon. Munitions stood in stacks underneath piles of cut foliage. Sixteen war drones rested in a line nearby and all around hundreds of second-children crouched in darkness. Skulker could feel the eyes of his fellows watching him. Though Skulker was valued, Harl did not much appreciate failure—pieces of Prador carapace scattered on the ground in this area were the result of other reports of failure brought to him.

"I encountered—"

Harl whirled round, all his attention abruptly focused on Skulker. "What is that on your carapace?"

"What?" Skulker tried to peer back with eye-palps he no longer possessed.

A tinny voice issued from somewhere just behind his visual turret. It took Skulker a moment to recognise it as that of the human male he earlier encountered. "It's a CTD gecko mine—yield of about five kilotonnes."

When the man stooped... doing something to his boot.

Skulker's shriek terminated in a blast that peeled back four square kilometres of jungle canopy and sunk a crater down to the bedrock. The blast did not utterly obliterate everything, for one drone shell, hollow, and glowing white-hot, quenched itself in an inland lake a hundred kilometres away.

While contemplatively running his finger in circles over the stippled copper surface of his new aug, Conlan gazed through the chainglass security screens to where a massive section of a storage buffer slowly slid on its maglev plates above the steel floor. He already knew that Marcus Heilberg was one of the designated grabship pilots for this run, but he had yet to crack the security protocol preventing him from finding this individual's location—information unobtainable by other, cruder means. Probably Marcus would still be in his quarters, since the run would not be proceeding for another twenty hours, which was just where Conlan wanted him to be. But where was his apartment?

The buffer section Heilberg had been assigned to transport, like a diagonally sliced piece of some huge chrome pipe, Conlan already knew all about. It could hold a charge in the terra-watt range. Already at half-charge, its laminar storage held enough energy to fry an in-system cruiser. They intended to position it just out from Gatepost Four ready for telefactor installation. Well, that was their plan.

His aug came through for him, giving him the location of Heilberg's apartment, and Conlan wondered at the superb efficiency of this device costing so small a sum even though fitted by a private surgeon. It first puzzled him to discover how little other augments could do in comparison to himself. How, for example, he was able to run a search-and-destroy program to wipe his old identity from many systems, and establish a new one. But then he became aware of AI searches being run through the planetary server, shortly before newsnet services brought out their story about Aubron Sylac's presence on Trajeen. Conlan realised he had deleted his old identity just in time, and now understood why his aug worked so well.

Viewing an internal model of the station, Conlan picked up his holdall and headed off to find Marcus Heilberg. He felt some relief to be moving again for he knew that the submind to the Trajeen Cargo Runcible AI, here on this station, would quickly begin running checks on anyone loitering suspiciously. Within minutes he stood before the correct door and rapped a knuckle against the door plate, before grinning up at the cam set above the door. After a moment the intercom came on and Marcus Heilberg enquired, "What the hell is it?"

Conlan held up one finger then stooped down to his holdall, removed a bottle of green brandy and held it up for inspection.

"Obviously not to be consumed now," he said. "We wouldn't want any accidents today. Jadris sent it by way of an apology. I'm to be your new copilot."

The door lock buzzed and clicked and Conlan stooped to pick up his holdall before entering. At that moment he noticed the blood soaked into the cuff of his jacket sleeve and felt a moment of disquiet—it was not like him to miss such details.

"What the hell is Jadris playing at?"

Aug.

Marcus Heilberg, a stooped, lanky individual with cropped black hair like Conlan's own, leant against a side table at the entryway from his kitchenette, pressing his fingertips against his aug, his expression puzzled.

"Can't seem to connect," he said.

Conlan scanned the apartment: blue floor moss, retro wooden furniture, pastel walls and picture screens repeating images of various spacecraft—probably those Heilberg once flew. The bedroom lay to the left, door open and no sign of movement inside. The kitchenette behind Heilberg was empty, the smell of frying bacon wafting out. The bathroom door also stood open, and from what he could see Conlan surmised there was no one in there. He strode forwards, the bottle held out to one side. "Bit of an unreliable bastard I gather, but at least his apology is worth something." He held the bottle higher, up-ended.

Fast—has to be fast.

Heilberg's eyes slid from Conlan to the bottle, just as it swept down against the side table. Frozen expression. Up with the jagged end, turning it slightly to present the most suitable edge. Momentary impact and resistance, then no resistance. The broken bottle sheared off two of Heilberg's fingers, one of which still clung by a strip of skin. It gouged down to his jawbone, sliced off most of his ear but, most importantly, cut Heilberg's aug from his head, which clattered bloodily to the floor as he staggered into the kitchenette doorjamb.

"Wha … why," the man managed, but Conlan did not stop to chat.

Face white, Heilberg turned and staggered into his kitchenette. Conlan kicked the man's feet out from under him and, discarding the bottle, came down in the centre of his back with his knee. Shoulder grip then and a swift jerk backwards. Heilberg's spine snapped with a gristly crunching. To be certain Conlan now took hold of his head and twisted it until he heard a similar sound. Then, having dropped the expiring man, he backed off, turned and swiftly checked the bathroom and bedroom. No one else home.

What and why?

Jadris asked similar questions while Conlan cut off his fingers to obtain the information he required. The answer was manifold, though Jadris did not hear it for shortly after that question Conlan strangled him with a length of optic cable. His reply should have been: because humans are no longer free, because the human race cannot achieve its manifest destiny while enslaved by the AI autocrat of Earth and all its minions. But really, all that was just the party line—the call to arms of the Separatist cause. Conlan possessed a more realistic view of his own motivations. He hated AIs. He hated their smug superiority, their rigid control over the activities of human beings, most specifically himself.

In the Organization, Conlan had been the top archetypal super hit man. People feared him, feared his name, and treated him with deference and awe. Throughout his bloody career he accumulated enough wealth to buy one of those small islands just off the Cogan peninsular. Retirement seemed a good idea, with maybe one or two hits a year to keep his hand in, for Conlan enjoyed his work. Then ECS, guided by its AIs, in just one day came down on the Organization like a hammer. Mass arrests followed, the ECS agents not too bothered about taking prisoners alive. The Boss, with Conlan's help, managed to escape in his private ship—or so Conlan thought before he saw the news feed concerning the tragic steamrolling of that ship by the moon, Vina. Conlan only escaped by dint of his contacts in the Trajeen Separatists. All his accounts were closed down and all his property seized. All he then owned was his Armani businesswear and a wallet full of New Carth shillings.

Over the ensuing years rigid ECS police control backed by the superior forensic and analytical abilities of the AIs, drove organized crime on Trajeen almost to extinction. Conlan was forgotten—to most people just a bad memory of a bad time. They turned his island into a damned resort visited by members of the runcible culture who lounged on his beach or visited his house—now opened as a small museum to past atrocities. Only the Separatists, with their rabid fanaticism and the cell structure of their organization, managed to cling to existence. He stayed with them, doing what he could, but it never seemed enough. Then came out-Polity financing from those promising to destroy ECS—an alien race who managed to build a star-spanning civilization without the interference of AIs. Next came this wonderful aug to put him in such a prime position. That these Prador promised to allow the Separatists free reign in the Polity, once ECS was pounded into mincemeat, Conlan doubted. But his hatred of ECS and the AIs took him beyond those doubts. He would rather see the Polity fragmented or ruled by aliens, than under the control of those damned machines. He was prepared to die fighting them which, he guessed, made him just as much a fanatic as the rest of the Separatists.

At age thirty-five, which was young for an ECS commando, Nelson felt determined to learn from the older veterans around him and not do anything stupidly naïve. Departing the lander on Grant's World, he gazed up at the rearing mound of bluish-red vegetable debris as his visor adjusted to the brightness. Glancing round at the rest of his squad he noticed they were now opening their visors. He checked the display down in the corner of his own and did the same.

"Shallow breaths," said Lithgow, "or we'll end up carrying you."

They moved away from the shuttle as it rapidly headed skyward again, and Nelson scanned the entire landing zone. Five square kilometres of jungle lay flattened by a planar bomb that had flung the wrecked vegetable matter into mounds all around the blast site. Probably because of these huge compost heaps, the air smelt of vinegar, ammonia and something putrid. Around the edge, just beyond them, he could see the pylons of autogun towers with twinned pulse-cannons tracking in gimbals across the jungle. Within the clearing stood a temporary city of domes and field tents. The domes were made by inflating hemispheres of monofilament and spraying on a mixture of a fast-setting epoxy and earth. The whole process had been conducted automatically by the base builder craft that plunged down here only two days ago. The troops, with their tents, had been arriving here ever since.

"Eyes up, here's the lieutenant," said Lithgow.

The Golem called Snake wore the shape of a man, but displayed little else in the way of human emulation. Nelson had seen many others like him lately, and Lithgow explained, "Emulation slows them down. They're not here to be nice and socially acceptable."

"Find yourselves a place and set up for the night. We move out at solstan 12.40." Snake tilted his head for a moment. "The whole camp breaks then because we'll be losing orbital cover by 15.00." He flicked a finger at them, then pointed towards the encampment before heading off with his sliding unhuman gait.

Lithgow, a burly woman who held the rank of sergeant, led the way to a clear area that could accommodate them. The troops shed their ridiculously large packs, which were pleasantly light in the three-quarter gees, and began pulling out their tents then stepping back while they auto-erected.

"Losing cover?" Nelson queried.

"One of those big fuck ships on its way I'd guess."

"Should we even be here then?"

"Should be smooth. They'll hit any large concentrations, but they don't want to trash this planet. It's got plenty of ocean cover and those big inland lakes—just the kind of place they like. That's why we're here."

Nelson figured that out and realised his chatter stemmed from him being wired. This would be his first action. For the others it would be no more than their second or third such fight with Prador troops and those hateful damned war drones of theirs. He turned away from Lithgow and set out his own tent to self-erect. It occurred to him, looking round, to wonder what troops from the past would think of this motley collection. They worked with a similar rank system as past armies because of the necessity of a chain of command, but there the similarity ended. They all wore fatigues of chameleon-cloth so seemed to be perpetually sliding in and out of existence as they moved about. Here greater emphasis was placed on individuality, this being an army of specialists. Nelson himself carried a heavy rifle that fired both laser and seeker bullets—he was the sniper of the group. Lithgow specialized in booby traps—a narrow field complemented by their other three explosives experts—one of whom carried tactical fission weapons in his pack. In their ranks were two code crackers, a linguist, an exobiologist and three medics who, as well as being able to deal with battlefield injuries, were also expert in specific fields: xenopathology, bioweapons and battle-stress analysis. And so it went. All carried laser carbines, grenades, missile launchers, mines—a whole panoply of death. The tac-officer, Lieutenant Snake, could override orders from above after assessing input from the various experts in the unit, and studying the exigent situation. Which was probably why he needed to be a Golem.

After stowing his gear in his tent, Nelson wondered what the hell to do next. Perhaps, he thought, I'm more like those troops from bygone days in that I need to be led. Lithgow sauntered over.

"Well, me and Genesh are going to hunt down a beer or two. Eat, drink and be merry as they say."

"What?"

"Never mind." Lithgow grabbed his shoulder and towed him after her.

The three of them walked on through the encampment, taking the most direct route towards the central domes. They stopped for a while to watch a telefactor operator, augs either side of her head, sitting cross-legged on the ground and putting two tripodal autoguns through their paces: squatting, running, and swivelling their twinned pulse-guns to pick out targets. The whole scene was weirdly reminiscent of some kind of dance.

"I wonder how well they'll do in jungle," commented Genesh.

They then passed a row of one-man ground tanks and

stacked pallets of explosive ammunition. Nelson jerked to a halt when he spotted what lay on the next pallet.

"What the fuck?"

Strapped to the pallet, folded up tight, rested a three-metre-long scorpion, thickly daubed with camouflage paint.

"Lithgow?" asked Genesh, and it gladdened Nelson to know he wasn't the only one to be stumped by this sight.

Abruptly the scorpion started to move. It raised its front end and Nelson saw, in place of mandibles and the usual insectile head, a row of launch tubes and two polished throats of some kind of energy weapon. It slowly spread its claws, like a man stretching after a long sleep. Then, almost negligently, it reached back and snipped through the steel straps securing it to the pallet, and rose up on its legs. It turned towards the three frozen troopers.

"Any of those lice-ridden crab fuckers nearby?" it asked in the rough voice of a terminal smoker.

Only Lithgow retained the presence of mind to reply. "Not at the moment." She pointed. "They've been dropping along the coast about a thousand kilometres that way."

"Best I go give a few the old rocket suppository." It came down off the pallet moving smooth as mercury and headed off in the direction Lithgow indicated.

"Would I appear too naïve if I asked what that was?" asked Nelson.

"That, my boy, was a Polity war drone. And if you ever thought AIs were sane and sensible, think again."

"But a useful lunatic to have on your side?" suggested Genesh.

Lithgow grimaced. "Yes, of course."

Eventually they found their way to one of the many commissaries. Here, like some alfresco café, tables and chairs were set out and umbrellas erected, though the umbrellas consisted of chameleon-cloth and when you sat beneath them that cloth palely matched the albescent sky. Lithgow and Nelson sat, while Genesh went off to find a few cold ones. Nelson noticed his companion staring at some nearby troops. He surreptitiously studied them himself, noting black webworms over their fatigues, heavy rifles much like his own strapped to a line of packs resting nearby, and that these troops wore utility belts ringed all the way around with gecko mines. Closer inspection revealed that many of them wore on their sleeves small gold buttons, and the occasionally large silvery ones, in the shape of crabs. One soldier rested his feet up on a table and a forage cap pulled low, but not low enough to conceal a chevron scar on his cheek.

"Who are they?" Nelson asked.

"Well, talking of useful lunatics to have on your side … those are the Avalonians."

Nelson shivered, despite the heat.

"Check out the guy with hat. See his scar?"

Nelson nodded.

"A Prador claw just missed taking off his head and snipped that in his cheek. He says it's a scar he intends to keep."

"You're saying that's—"

"Yup. You're looking at Jebel U-cap Krong."

Nelson eyed this slim and apparently not too noteworthy man. He knew what the "U-cap" stood for. Who didn't? Jebel up-close-and-personal Krong. Now Nelson remembered what the buttons represented. The gold ones were for second-children and the larger, platinum ones, were for first-children. To earn such a button you needed to get close enough to a Prador to plant a gecko mine on its carapace, and blow it to pieces. Krong wore two ruby buttons because he changed the counting method—his own sleeve having become too overloaded. Ten golds equalled one platinum, and ten platinum buttons equalled one ruby.

Genesh returned with litre steins of chilled beer, which they sipped while they talked. Nelson could not help but steal glances at the Avalonians and their leader. He felt some disappointment when Jebel and his troops abruptly stood and moved to take up their packs, before heading off towards the landing field. But he grinned to himself thinking how, for a little while, he sat in the presence of a legend. He did not realise he was about to become part of a legend himself: the planet the Prador ground forces could not take, the one they finally bombarded from orbit with antimatter missiles. Grant's World ... the war grave.

The mask melded to his face like cool porridge, and after a moment it matched his facial expressions to perfection. It was old tech, but nonetheless effective. Eyeing the image of Marcus Heilberg staring back at him from the mirror, Conlan grinned, then reached into his top pocket to remove Heilberg's aug, still connected to his own by the length of optic cable he used to strangle Jadris. He long ago learnt that it took more strain than that ensuing from a strangulation to damage this grade of optic cable—strange the facts you picked up along the way.

His own aug having processed the download from the other aug, he now knew all he needed to know about Heilberg's next run—all the flight and security protocols, all the codes. Only one thing remained. He turned from the mirror, stooped to remove a small brushed aluminium box from his holdall, then headed for the kitchenette.

Heilberg's head now lay in a pool of his own blood. Conlan stared at the mess for a moment, then took hold of the corpse's ankle and dragged the body into the main living area, smearing a gory trail behind. Stretching Heilberg's right arm out, he placed the aluminium box down beside it and popped the box open. Most people wore their augs on the left-hand side of their heads if they were right-handed and vice versa, and most right-handed people used that hand on palm-readers. Of course, the situation being otherwise with Heilberg's right hand up against his aug, Conlan would have waited until he lowered it before using the bottle. He did not want this hand damaged.

From the box he removed a chainglass scalpel and cut around the wrist, careful not to sever any tendons. This done he used a small hook to stretch out the larger, severed blood vessels and place small clamps on them. Now the tendons, which he stretched out individually and clamped before cutting. The ends of the tendons leading up into the arm snapped out of sight, but those leading into the hand, because of the clamps, remained accessible to him. He continued his surgery, cutting the radius and ulna bones with a small electric saw and slicing remaining flesh. Soon the hand separated, and he set about replacing the clamps on the tendons with specially designed bayonet fittings and those on the blood vessels with similar though hollow fittings. He sprayed a sealant over the raw end to close off the smaller blood vessels and capillaries. This done, he stared at the hand for a moment before rolling up his sleeve and pressing four points in a particular sequence on his forearm. His right hand flopped—all feeling instantly departing it. A quick slice about the syntheskin around his wrist gave him access to the specially designed interface plug between his artificial arm—attached at his shoulder—and artificial hand. He detached the hand, then set about inserting the bayonets into their various ports, before finally pushing the bones into their central clamps—replacing his artificial hand with Heilberg's. He then wrapped around syntheskin tape to cover the join.

Now came the critical part as he waited for the interface

port to make its connections. From a small reservoir within his forearm, artificial blood, at the required temperature and pressure, cycled through the hand. Servomotors would pull on the tendons. There was no doubt that both these operations would certainly work. The one that might fail was the injection of copper composite whiskers through flesh to the major muscles in the hand, since he did not have the time or equipment to make nerve connections. He waited, studying a readout screen situated in the aluminium box. When it finally gave him the go-ahead he flexed the hand, then closed it into a fist. Not quite right, and no feeling, no feedback, but it would serve.

Eighteen hours now until the flight. Conlan settled himself in Heilberg's apartment, first eating the bacon cooked under the grill, then attempting to sleep in Heilberg's bed. Time dragged. Conlan dared not take a pill to knock himself out, so spent an uncomfortable six hours in the bed. Later he showered, and wearing a towelling robe once belonging to the corpse—now wrapped in a sheet and shoved out of sight behind the sofa—he tried out Heilberg's disc collection. Finally he found more interesting entertainment in the intricacies of his own aug. Prior to leaving, he changed into a spare flight overall belonging to Heilberg. It wasn't easy with only one truly workable hand, but he did not want any blood on this clothing again. He placed his artificial hand in the man's flight bag, then took it up and headed off to find his grabship, glad to be going since the smell in Heilberg's apartment was becoming none too pleasant.

Immanence observed that the radiation levels were high, as was the quantity of orbital debris not present some months before. There were still some ECS ships limping around the system, but mainly they were just trying to survive. Captain Shree, in his ship parked geostationary above Grant's World along with four troop carriers, did not concern himself about them. The other, smaller Prador ships were conducting the cleanup operation. Shree's concern was for the planet below, and the damnable forces there.

"They are as difficult to remove as a ship louse bored into a shell joint," the captain complained. "I personally have lost two hundred second-children and three first-children, and have necessarily taken some third-children out of storage to raise to the next level. Surface Arm have lost nearly a million second-children, hundreds of first-children, and nearly twenty thousand war drones. The enemy has now established a runcible down there from which we keep picking up U-space interference, but cannot find, and they keep bringing in new forces. Unless we do find it, we cannot win."

"I am here to relay new orders from the King," Immanence told the other captain, revelling in his authority. "We will win here."

Shree made a gobbling sound, probably assuming this to be one of those "sort it out or die" orders from the Prador monarch, and now wondering if there might be any way he could pin failure on Immanence who was now the ranking Prador adult here.

The hierarchical system of the Prador had been medieval and vicious for centuries. The King ruled by dint of being the nastiest and most conniving of them all, and managed to maintain his rule by setting all those below him against each other and ruthlessly crushing any single Prador who became too powerful. Those below him determined their ranking by endless complicated infighting and brief alliances that usually ended in bloody betrayals. The captains of dreadnoughts, like Shree and Immanence, were of the highest rank, having accumulated enough wealth and power to buy into the resources and industrial capacity the King controlled. Those lower down the scale captained smaller ships or provided troops, while those lower still ran the infrastructure of Prador society. All adult Prador ruled huge families with an absolute power the worst human dictators would have envied. In this complicated hierarchical structure, Shree lay a stratum below Immanence. Captain Immanence allowed Shree to assume the worst for a while before putting him right.

"The King has decided that expending resources here to take this world would delay the push into the Polity for too long." Shree fell silent. Immanence now opened up the communication to all the Prador adults in the system, and all those first-children commanders whose fathers were back within the Kingdom. "All land forces are to immediately withdraw from the planet. You have five days in which to comply. The ban on tactical fission weapons is now raised so you may use them to cover your retreat. We no longer have a use for this place."

Shree got the idea. "It seems a shame. This world would have made a pleasant addition to the Kingdom."

Immanence guessed the other captain had considered the possibility of staking claim to some portion of Grant's World. He himself would have liked to have done the same. It sometimes felt a little crowded back in the Kingdom and with space like this it would be possible for any adult to greatly extend his family using the same massive crèche systems some adults used to provide second- and first-child fodder for ground combat. Increasing the number of children would logically lead to increases in wealth, industrial capacity, *power*. And maybe then, from such a position, said adult could contemplate a little regicide. Perhaps this too was a reason for the King's decision about this place.

During the ensuing five days, Immanence dropped small

sensor drones to observe the retreat and evacuation. He watched retreating Prador cramming onto AG platforms and sliding low over jungle canopy while a line of detonation flashes behind them momentarily blanked vision. Massive fireballs rose and shockwaves spread in perfect rings as they flattened jungle, which poured smoke flat to the ground before igniting violently. He saw human troops running and burning, then being swept up in ground winds like all the rest of the burning debris. Thousands of square kilometres of jungle burned, along with those human fighters occupying it. But in the air things were not going so well.

Immanence watched retreating Prador scramble quickly aboard troop transports at the assigned assembly points. Automatic guns and missile launchers covered them there, but not when the transports laboured into orbit. They were guarded by gunboats mounting lasers and missile launchers, and by spherical Prador war drones run by the transplanted cerebral and nerve tissue of second-children. But Polity AI war drones came in fast—weird machines often fashioned in the shape of living creatures. Immanence observed one such formation of things like silvery lice or chouds and shelled molluscs. They approached in a line, then broke, accelerating on fusion drives to employ a seemingly random attack pattern, which in instants resulted in two gunboats dropping, burning, from the sky and a line of four Prador war drones detonating one after another. Remaining Prador defence forces thoroughly engaged, a Polity drone in the shape of some segmented arthropod zipped up underneath the transport, clung for a moment, then darted away. The detonation of the mine it placed blew the transport to small pieces, the blast wave slamming into defenders suddenly finding their opponents gone. Over two thousand Prador ground troops were incinerated.

But it seemed the humans and the AIs were beginning

to register the change in tactics and were pulling their own forces back on the surface. Analysing this retreat, Immanence narrowed down the position of the runcible to the north of one of the main continents. He targeted the centre of that spread of jungle. Some Prador forces still remained within the zone, but the loss would not be unacceptable. He launched a single antimatter missile, maximum acceleration all the way down. It cut an orange streak of fire through atmosphere, as it burnt away its ablation shield, and hammered into the ground. A mountain rose then flew apart in a growing sphere of annihilating fire. A fire storm spread, instantly, across thousands of square kilometres of jungle, and the ensuing shockwave peeled up the topsoil from bedrock. From orbit he observed a massive disk-shaped cloud spread above the detonation site. Beyond, the devastation spread almost like a pyroclastic flow. Within minutes a million square kilometres of jungle turned into something like the surface of a world closely orbiting a sun. No sign, thereafter, of any U-space interference. The runcible was gone.

The evacuation was all but complete on the fourth day, though heavy losses were inflicted by Polity war drones, which carried the fight all the way up into orbit—the drones attacking until depleting all their weaponry, then slamming themselves as hard and fast as possible into any vulnerable Prador ship. At this point Immanence contacted Shree to say, "Now."

Antimatter missiles rained down on the planet, each one, at a minimum, causing devastation the same as that caused by the one Immanence had used to destroy the runcible. Within hours it became impossible to see the continents from orbit, for the atmosphere filled with smoke, steam and debris. Tsunamis slammed around the world washing thousands of kilometres inshore. A fault line reactivated three hundred kilometres inshore of one continent, and dropped everything behind it five metres into the ocean. Some inactive volcanoes exploded violently into action, one active volcano went out. Immanence supposed that, after a winter lasting a century or so, the jungle might return. It would take millions of years before this place evolved large life forms again. All but maybe a few of the large, alien life forms down there were dead.

"Satisfactory," said Immanence. "Now, Shree, with a little stopover to remove a Polity transfer station—a small matter, no more than a nibbling louse—you will accompany me to a system the humans name Trajeen, where we will seize from them a runcible that is not planet-based."

"Do we have need of such things?" Shree asked.

"Some of the technology may come in useful, but if not, what matter? Another human world there awaits our attention."

"What's with Jadris?" said the new copilot. "He can't just do that at the last moment—the AI wants those buffers in position and ready for fitting straight after the test."

"Too much green brandy?" Conlan suggested.

The woman looked at him with slight puzzlement and Conlan rather suspected his mimicking of Heilberg's voice might be wrong. "What did you hear?" he asked.

She shrugged. "He auged in to opt out of this flight, saying he was sick, then he took his aug offline, so he must be unwell to not be taking calls. But it's not like him to be so irresponsible."

Conlan studied her as she moved off ahead of him. She was an attractive woman with a bald skull, fine coffee skin and an evident athleticism that did not detract from her femininity. But then Polity cosmetic surgery made it possible for anyone to be attractive. Maybe she had been born an ugly troglodyte with warts, bad breath and suppurating acne.

At the security gate into the flight bay, she stepped ahead of him to press her hand against the palm reader, then walked through. He glanced up, noting the drone hanging Damoclean overhead, and placed Heilberg's hand against the reader. Nothing happened, no alarms and no sudden activity from the drone, and he walked through trying not to show any reaction.

"Green brandy you say?" she asked him.

Conlan scanned the four ships presently resting in the huge bay and felt a brief moment of panic. All four of them were grabships stripped of their claws, and all three held runcible buffer sections dogged under their forward cockpits. He had no idea which one was Heilberg's. Fortunately the copilot moved on ahead of him. He wished she would stop talking. He didn't know her name or what her association with Heilberg might be. They could have been lovers, they might have shared in-jokes and all that sad paraphernalia born of friendships.

Rather than head for any of the ships she turned to the right, and only when he called up schematics of this area in his aug did he realise she was heading for the changing room.

Idiot!

It would have looked hugely suspicious if he'd climbed aboard without donning a spacesuit first. Though these ships were very rugged, safety procedures on what was effectively a construction site required crew to wear spacesuits.

Within the changing area others were stripping off clothing before open lockers, hanging the clothing inside and then donning their suits. Relief again when he saw that each locker bore a name stencilled on the door. He walked up to Heilberg's and pressed his hand against the reader beside it. Nothing happened. Conlan just stood there swallowing dryly.

"Is that bloody thing still playing up?" asked the copilot.

"So it would seem," he replied, not knowing what to do next. She provided the answer for him by reaching over and thumping the wall beside the plate as she passed. The door popped open. Conlan felt a great gratitude towards—he checked the name on the locker she came to a halt before—Anna Vasco.

Conlan stripped off his clothing and donned the spacesuit, surreptitiously making adjustments so it fitted him properly. He glanced aside at Anna, and seeing her utterly naked, tanned and sleek as she pulled out her suit, felt a surge of excitement. She glanced at him, noting his attention, and, rather deliberately he felt, dropped her suit then bent over, with her naked behind towards him, to pick it up. Of course, he knew, by the standards of general humanity, that between his ears lay a twisted ugly mess. He was a psychopath, and he knew that his heterosexual wiring had fused with other parts of his psyche. Hence the prospect of killing a sexually attractive woman excited him in an entirely different way from how he felt about Jadris and Heilberg. Unfortunately, he could not pander to the part of himself requiring the act to be protracted. The woman must die quickly. Such a shame.

Suitably attired, and with their bowl helmets tucked under their arms, they headed out towards the ships. Again Conlan let Anna take the lead, and thus discovered that Heilberg's ship lay second from the left. They boarded, stooping through the cramped body of the vessel, which was racked out and packed with the kinds of hand tools Conlan often employed for purposes other than those intended. He smiled at a row of electric screwdrivers and remembered how it once took him many hours and many hundreds of self-tapping screws to kill one man, and the subsequent long-running joke in the Organization that if you crossed Conlan you were screwed.

In the bulbous chainglass cockpit Anna took the copilot's seat while Conlan strapped himself in where Heilberg once sat. Of course Anna's presence was for the same reasons as the spacesuits—a precautionary measure—and having little to do, she chattered. Conlan kept his replies monosyllabic so as not to offer any encouragement while they waited for their slot. Soon the two ships ahead of Heilberg's moved through the ship lock at the end of the bay, and his turn came. The maglev in the bay automatically drew the ship into the lock, the entry doors sealing behind. High-speed pumps screamed up to full function, their sound gradually receding as they removed from the lock the medium for carrying sound. The outer doors opened with a puff of residual atmosphere, and maglev, and the station's spin, threw the grabship out into vacuum. Showing confident professionalism, Conlan started the vessel's fusion engine—pointed away from the station—and made the required corrections to bring it on course for the cargo runcible.

"Is there something wrong with your hand?" Anna asked.

Difficult to hide, and her question would have been the first of many. One more task, then, for Heilberg's hand. He straightened it and chopped back hard, smashing Anna's nasal bones up into her head. She snorted a spray of blood all over the cockpit screen as she choked into silence. Conlan inspected the hand. The force of the blow had torn it from the interface clamps and it now stuck out at an odd angle from his forearm. He removed it, and replaced it with his own artificial one—glad of the return of feeling and sensitivity, for he would need all his faculties for what he intended. But before he set about preparing for that task, he unstrapped Anna from her seat and dragged her into the back. He found her presence distracting.

5.

Which they ate with a runcible spoon–

He managed to ignore it at first, the people patting him on the back or grasping his hand and saying, "It's great to meet you," or "Thank you for what you're doing," or simply staring. But now as he sat sipping a glass of the local brew—something called greenwine—at one of the bars in the arcade leading to the main runcible complex, he began to become a little irritated. "Christ! You think they'd be used to seeing soldiers by now."

Urbanus, who sipped a glass of cranberry vodka just to be sociable and because a fuel cell in his body could utilize it to power him, emulated an amused smile and gazed up at the glass ceiling of the arcade. "Are you going to tell him, Lindy, or shall I?"

"I think we should let him find out for himself, don't you?" Lindy replied. She glanced back into the bar itself where numerous customers had gathered since their arrival, and kept peering out at them. Then she bit her lip and nodded to a screen display affixed amidst ivy on the outer wall of the bar.

"What are you two—" Jebel turned towards the screen. "That's Grant's World… fucking Prador."

The scene depicted a camouflaged second-child fleeing through jungle. Something familiar about that, but then

Jebel had seen many fleeing Prador. He let his gaze stray away and saw that a group of people now gathered on the main concourse were looking towards the bar. When they saw he had spotted them, some of them grinned, nodded and moved off. Others stayed to point out the bar to others. Jebel was beginning to get the creepy feeling it was him they were pointing to, and it made him feel nervy.

"Excuse me, sir."

Jebel spun round spilling some greenwine down his shirt front. His hand dropped to the thin-gun holstered on his belt. Then he lowered his gaze to a small boy standing before him—a kid in ersatz fatigues, a toy pistol on his belt and a pet lizard clinging to his shoulder.

"Hey," said Jebel, "I'm no recruiting officer."

The boy did not seem to know how to reply to this, so instead looked towards a woman standing a few paces back, clutching a holocamera. She held the device up questioningly. Jebel supposed the kid, who was obviously into militaria, wanted a recording of himself with some soldiers. He shrugged and waved a hand obligingly. Boy moved up beside him as the woman, probably his mother, raised the recorder.

"Can you stand by me?" the boy asked.

Feeling rather foolish, Jebel stood with his hand on the boy's shoulder.

"What's your name?" he asked.

"Alan," the boy replied.

"So you want to be a soldier?"

"I want to be like you," the boy replied, staring up at him wide-eyed.

Like adults throughout history Jebel then just stood there unable to think of anything else to say. Certainly the boy would not want to be like Jebel, but how to explain that to him? Finally the woman came over.

"Thank you for that." She held up her holocamera exposing a fingerprint and gene reader plate. "Could you verify it, please? I know it's an imposition, but there are sure to be fakes."

"Well … yeah, sure." Jebel pressed his thumb against the plate until the device beeped.

"We'll leave you in peace now—I expect you get a lot of this." Hand on her boy's shoulder, she moved away. The boy kept looking back at Jebel, still wide-eyed.

Jebel sat, not quite sure what to think.

"Of course," said Urbanus, "the lizard on his shoulder is a gecko—they've become quite a fashionable pet."

Gecko.

"Worryingly dense, our great leader," Lindy added.

With interminable slowness, realisation surfaced in Jebel's consciousness. He understood then that, on some level, he already knew. He turned and looked at the bar's screen and observed airborne shots of a glowing crater surrounded by burning jungle.

"Recorded by the AIs, war drones," said Jebel, then turning to Urbanus, "and you?"

The Golem nodded. "Those were my instructions. The Polity needs good news of victories right now, and there's damned few of them. It also needs heroes."

"I'm not sure I—" Shadows abruptly fell across their table. Jebel looked up to see four floating holocams jockeying for position above him.

"Looks like the Trajeen newsnets just found out," said Lindy.

"I won't stay here for this," said Jebel.

"No need," Urbanus replied, "I've just been informed that our services are required elsewhere, if you are willing."

"Where?" Jebel asked.

Urbanus pointed up through the roof of the arcade, at an

object only just visible in the sky.

Standing upon the bridge of one of the utility ships available to the runcible project, Moria gazed through a chainglass screen at the nearby Boh runcible hanging in silhouette before the gas giant: a small thorny object skating above banded colour and omnipotent indifference. She rubbed at the back of her neck. The tension, just bearable during the transit here, seemed to have stretched all her muscles and turned her spine into a rod. Her stomach also felt full of swirling oil and she'd not eaten for ten hours. But the excitement was gone. Moria acknowledged to herself that the war removed the gloss of discovery and adventure from it all. Everyone was distracted by the constant bad news, and only recently were people becoming frightened. Staff were also being seconded away by ECS to work in the big shipyards, and many of those remaining worried about kin either involved in the conflict or living on worlds closer to the front line. How could anyone feel excited about the runcible project now that the Prador were killing millions, taking world after world, and smashing Polity dreadnoughts like a steamroller tracking over walnuts. Moria shook her head and tried to return to the moment.

When they first approached, she was able to discern the smaller objects spreading away from the runcible itself, some of them towed by grabships, some moving under their own power, and some being shifted by stripped-down drive motors bolted into place. To evacuate the runcible about half of the infrastructure—all the scaffolds and extraneous rubbish and all the occupied accommodation units—was moved to a lower orbit, and since then boosted around the other side of Boh, that being probably the safest place to move them, in the permitted time, should there be any mishaps.

U-space com established between Trajeen and Boh, Moria could call up a real-time view of events back at the other runcible. There a different procedure was used. Rather than detach paraphernalia from around the runcible, the staff were evacuated to Trajeen. The runcible itself, driven far out from the planet by five big fusion motors, represented less of a danger than the Boh one since at that end any mishaps would not be so cataclysmic. Now in deep dark, with Trajeen a distant blue marble, that runcible waited. And a hundred kilometres away from it, the big cargo carrier stood ready: one kilometre long and half a kilometre wide, that final distance extended by old-style balanced U-space engine nacelles and a third very old U-navigation nacelle—they did not want to use a new vessel for this. The ship's holds were filled with asteroidal rock to bring its mass up for the test. Neither humans nor AIs occupied it—George, or rather the larger part of him back at the Trajeen runcible, would guide it remotely through the gate.

"As well as data gathering and collation at this end," said George, standing beside her, "I want you to model the entire test."

"Well, thanks for that," Moria checked the time to the test in her aug, "but a little more notice would have been nice."

"As we have thus far discovered: it is only when you are under pressure that the more esoteric programs and functions of your aug are revealed."

"How much more processing space do you think it has, and how fast do you think it can operate?" she asked.

"This is what we will find out. But if you do run out of space and speed," George pointed towards the gas giant, "there are five server satellites in orbit to which you can apply for more." He glanced at her, and as he did so the codes she could use for this arrived in her aug. "Any more capacity you might require has been prepaid and so held open for you."

She turned and faced him. "So tell me, what's being tested here, the cargo runcible or my aug?"

"Both," George replied, still staring out into vacuum. He then frowned and continued, "The current war situation being what it is, it seems likely this project will shortly be relocated. Also, augs such as yours might be useful to the war effort—perhaps more so than a working cargo runcible."

"But you'd need Sylac for that."

"Sylac was apprehended on Cheyne III and is currently in transit to Titan, where he will be working for ECS."

Moria absorbed that, then replayed what George had just said. "Hang on … relocated. We'll not be able to move these runcibles."

"The research will be relocated." Now George turned to face her. "These runcibles will be destroyed before the Prador arrive here."

For a moment Moria was stunned. Yes, the war was impinging and taking all the excitement out of the project, but only now did the reality truly strike her. "They are coming here?"

"Unless we gain some unexpected advantage, the battle line will cross the Trajeen system in two months time. Since we came out here," he nodded towards Boh, "evacuation and defence programs have been instituted. But it seems likely Trajeen will either be occupied by the Prador or rendered inert. ECS will not be able to halt the Prador advance until the shipyards are all fully functional."

Rendered inert.

And there, she realised, the difference between George and a normal human being. She should never forget that he was essentially an AI submind in a human shell, and along with all the other Polity AIs directed an interstellar war like some kind of chess game in which worlds were pawns.

"Will we win, do you think?" she asked.

"Define 'win,' " said George, staring at her steely eyed, then he seemed to relent. "The Polity will certainly survive, but in what form or after sustaining how much damage is debatable. At least our course is clear."

"Clear?"

"We are defending ourselves from an alien aggressor with seemingly no regard for the lives of our citizens. This is our first encounter with them and we have given them no reason for their aggression. We are fighting to survive not to defend or impose some political ideology, nor to maintain or gain some economic advantage ... as has been the human custom. Those who fight will suffer few moral qualms."

"Oh, that's okay then."

"It is time for you to begin modelling the test," he told her, expression bland.

After that?

She felt like just telling him to bugger off, but then took a grip upon herself. Cold in his summation of the situation George might be. Cold in their plans might be the Polity AIs. But the luxury of emotional breast-beating would not win this kind of merciless, industrialized conflict. What would win it would be the efficient construction and deployment of weapons, the measured choices in the development of technologies, intricate battle-planning to the advantage of the Polity as a whole, calculation, working the numbers. Very few AIs bothered to play roulette, those that did always won.

"Did you hear me?" George asked.

"Yes, I heard."

Moria began with the basic real-time virtual model of the two gates, distances truncated to fit within the compass of her perception. She then created underlying gravity, system vector/energy and U-space coordinates maps. But these were only the parchment on which she painted the rest. Recalling from memspace the models she had already created of the two runcibles' energy systems, she began running predicted function, perpetually updated by actual function—the delay measured in microseconds. Soon she observed warp initiation. Between the five gateposts of each runcible the cusps formed: each like the meniscus of a soap bubble. Slowly then, the five horn-shaped posts began to slide apart, opening like iris doors, stretching each cusp across vacuum. The cargo ship's fusion drive ignited like a white star and the vessel now began to accelerate towards the Trajeen gate.

"0.0004532 disparity between G2 and 3 here," she noted.

"Already noted," George replied. "You now have access. Make the necessary correction."

Moria felt a moment of pure terror as channels opened from the Boh runcible to her aug, and she found herself taking a mental step back as appalling data flows overwhelmed her. She applied to the Boh servers and processing space opened. She began running the calculations to superpose her model on reality and find the required corrections. She created and collapsed formulae in her mind, in her aug, quickly working her way through the problem. Then came the ecstasy of squirting the solution over to the runcible. A few brief squirts from the runcible's attitude jets closed the disparity and shortly her superposed model matched.

The five horns now completely separated, spreading the meniscus across a kilometre of space. Between them, the edges of that strange severance of realspace blurred out and away, spilling Hawking radiation into vacuum. However, Moria soon recognised an untoward energy drain in the system, and put online two more reactors at the Boh runcible. George did not instruct her to do this, but he made no objection. She saw that the larger part of him, at Trajeen, did the same.

"I now give you total control of the Boh outer gate."

Shit! Fuck!

Now the vessel reached the Trajeen gate and went through, gone in an instant. A microsecond of calculation as the buffer feedback figures came through. Precisely the correct amount of energy applied at the meniscus. Calculations collapsing beyond it. A blurring, negative state, U-space calculus, a glimpse of understanding: *everything there and everything here, matter just rucked up space-time and time itself a mere parenthesis...*

The cargo vessel flashing through the gate, backwards, twisted out of shape and trailing fire. A thousand kilometres beyond the gate it abruptly decelerated, yet none of its engines could be working to do that. Then it just came apart as if somehow all its components transformed into wet clay. Metal and chunks of asteroidal rock slowly spread out, breaking down further until micro-debris formed a sphere which began to be distorted by Boh's gravity. Moria felt as if someone flash-froze her brain then cracked it with a hammer. She groaned and went down on her knees.

"What went wrong?" George: calm, analytical.

"I don't know!" she yelled.

"That is a shame. You still have a long way to go."

She knew, instantly, that he was not talking about just her.

During the weeks of travel through U-space, Immanence reviewed his family's present status in the Kingdom and made plans for further expansion upon his return by deciding on which alliances he should make or break, which other Prador to bring down if not assassinate—though the assassination of Prador adults was never easy—and by working on scenarios based on all the new things he had learned since the war's beginning. But such plans remained skeletal at best, and protean, for who knew what advantages or disadvantages he might own over the next few years, or how many of his allies or enemies might be destroyed, or how their positions might change? It was the ability to adjust his plans to changing circumstances that had raised him to his present position, and he relished the prospect of further rapid change. However, after a time such planning in a vacuum palled, and he turned his attention to history recordings—private and public—then to weapons design, the formulation of new poisons, possible application of enslaved humans ... but steadily lost interest in each subject as he worked through it.

The entertainments available to him in his sanctum finally all but exhausted, Immanence decided to take a tour of his ship before its arrival at the next target. He summoned both Vagule and Gnores, and the second-child XF-326 along with a random selection of that one's contemporaries. The two first-children arrived before the others outside the closed doors to the sanctum and Immanence watched them through the corridor cam system. Gnores moved to the fore and carefully watched the doors. Vagule shoved him aside, and when Gnores raised his claws, Vagule quickly smacked him hard across the visual turret. Gnores hesitated—not being that much smaller than Vagule—but the other having been appointed Prime by Immanence forced his decision. He squealed obligingly and backed off.

Now the second-children arrived, led by XF-326 who, Immanence noted, with his new privileges providing him better nutrition that Immanence also ordered dosed with certain hormones, was growing fast. The second-children, clambering over each other behind where XF-326 halted a safe distance from the two first-children, were all about the same size. His size lay between that of them and Vagule and Gnores. Immanence understood why XF-326 held back. His recent growth spurts would have weakened his carapace and a blow administered by either of the two first-children might result in serious injury. Immanence rose up on his grav-motors and swung towards the doors, ordering them open as he slid towards them.

Much scrambling, pushing and shoving ensued as his children realised he actually intended to leave the sanctum. The second-children were fine staying in the corridor all about him, there being room for them. As Immanence turned into the wide oblate-section corridor, perfect for his large carapace, he noted that XF-326 assumed the safe position directly underneath the rear of his carapace—safe so long as the captain did not decide to shut off his grav-motors, which he was known to do. Vagule and Gnores necessarily scrambled ahead, scuttling sideways so they could keep their father in clear view, clattering their back ends against the rough walls, loosening weed and sending ship lice scuttling.

"I want to see how you are progressing with these humans," Immanence told them.

"We have four recently implanted, and we are seeing how they progress before doing any more," Vagule informed him.

"I am aware of the current status of your research, Vagule. I want to see the entire process. Bring up another four and show me."

"We were thinking of trying spider thralls next," piped up Gnores.

Immanence observed Vagule's mandibles grinding and knew that Gnores would pay for that impertinence later.

"Why spider thralls?" Immanence asked.

Gnores replied, "With a less traumatic installation we were hoping... were expecting... that is—"

Vagule interrupted, "Even with all the support systems, full coring kills them within a few days. We are gradually learning about their autonomous nervous system, but we need to learn more to know what can be safely retained or discarded. Using spider thralls we are hoping they will live longer and thus provide us with more time to gather data."

Very good, thought Immanence. Vagule already understood that though the truth might result in some unpleasant punishment, lies, though delaying it, would result in punishment more severe.

"How many have died so far?"

"As a result of installation, fifty-three. A further eight have died in the holding area from injuries suffered during capture. We have also discovered that feeding them can be a problem. At present they are refusing to eat their own kind, though that might change should they become sufficiently hungry."

"And?"

"I would rather try them on other foods, since waiting until they are starving would result in them being weakened and ill and less able to sustain thrall implantation."

"Very well. Try them on our stores of meat and check their requirements for supplements. These humans are omnivores, remember, so may require certain minerals from vegetative matter."

At the end of the corridor they reached a shaft down which Vagule and Gnores scurried. Immanence slid into it, the second-children scuttling all around him and descending using footholds in the rough wall of the shaft. Immanence dropped slowly in the lower gee, his grav-motors countering the plates at the shaft bottom to halt him a few metres from the floor. The procession continued until they reached a sealed chamber much like the captain's sanctum. Vagule opened the doors for him and ducked inside. Immanence followed, scenting alien blood and flesh and the other smells concomitant with human life, and death. In the chamber he turned, surveying the humans upon whom Vagule experimented.

Twelve of them were clamped along one wall. To his left lay a stack of about twenty corpses—failures. Of the twelve, he could see by the readouts on the hexagonal screens above, five were dead. He eyed a rack of spider thralls, then another rack containing the larger thrall hardware required after a full coring. Perhaps something even smaller should be made? Immanence filed the thought for later attention as he now surveyed surgical equipment dipped in bins of sterilizing grease and two surgical robots standing off to one side. These dark metal shells conformed to the foreparts, visual turret and underside of a first-child. Many recessed pit controls inside took their claws and manipulatory hands, whilst to the fore spread many jointed, precision limbs, each ending in surgical tools.

"Remove the corpses and bring in four replacements," Immanence instructed. He then gestured his claw towards XF-326. "You, bring one of them over and feed me."

Under orders from Vagule, Gnores took some of the second-children off to collect four living humans, while Immanence kept a greedy eye on XF-326. The second-child closed its claw into the ribcage of one corpse, swiftly dragged it over and methodically began to dismember it, passing up pieces to Immanence's mandibles. As he crunched up a severed hand and forearm, the captain contemplated what enabled him to eat such fare. The rugged Prador digestive system could extract nutriment from a stone—this being a known method of survival in some situations. While eating he realised that decay improved the taste, probably because bacteria in the ship were partially breaking down the alien flesh. Even so, the captain pondered the quirks of evolutionary biology that resulted in something that tasted so good.

Gnores returned with the four humans who were, until they entered this chamber, docile and mainly inactive. However, two of them began yelling and babbling human speech. Immanence guessed they found the scene somewhat distracting. Sending a command to one of his sanctum chouds he ran the speech through a translator then directly back to him, but it revealed nothing of relevance, just many questions concerning their fate, occasional threats, and vague references to some human deity. He studied the humans while Gnores and the second-children began stripping off their filthy clothing. They were difficult to tell apart but now Immanence knew enough about their anatomy to identify one male, two females and a younger version that was probably the human equivalent to a second-child, though he could not guess at what its sex might be. Strange creatures. What was the purpose of that thick mat of hair on their heads, some form of protection perhaps? Why were two of them emptying their bowels—surely in a dangerous situation it would be better not to leave a scent that could be tracked? What purpose was served by piercing the body here and there with pieces of rare metals decorated with cut gems? Why those vulnerable external genitalia on the men and those ridiculously inflated mammary glands on the women? Immanence realised he had much yet to learn, should he be interested enough.

Vagule inserted himself into the back hollow of a surgical robot while Gnores and the others clamped the humans to the wall. The babble soon ceased when human-specific drugs were injected and feed-lines attached to their veins.

The spider thralls—each leggy device no larger than a human thumb—were installed via splits in the thick muscle on either side of the back of their necks. One of the humans—the child—for no immediately apparent reason died during this procedure.

"How many do we have left?" Immanence asked, his manner slightly bored now as he turned back towards the doors, though through his chouds he spied on the data streams from the thralls.

"Six hundred and twenty," Vagule replied, backing out of the surgical robot.

"I will be expecting some measure of success by the time that figure drops to five hundred and sixty," Immanence told him. "And I will be most displeased by failure."

"As you order," Vagule replied, sagging slightly.

Gnores, however, immediately perked up at this, as did XF-326. They all knew precisely what Immanence meant by it: that some time soon the opportunity for promotion might arise, after one terminal demotion.

While the grabship flew on automatic towards the Trajeen cargo runcible, Conlan scratched between his aug and his ear to lift the edge of his mask, pressed a control no larger than a pinhead and felt the mask sag on his face. After a moment all its edges lifted and he peeled it away and dropped it beside his seat. Then he studied the grabship's controls.

Though a pilot carried out the main task of launching the vessel and much of the final manoeuvring to position its load, certain safety protocols were also functioning, and he was constantly monitored. Should he become ill, or die, the runcible AI could take control to guide the ship out of danger and back to base. Also, if the vessel deviated from its mission plan, the AI would be alerted, and could again take control. For example, if the pilot took it into his head to ram the ship into one of the runcible gateposts, the AI would swiftly put a stop to that.

Subverting such systems was no easy task with the usual hardware, which was why Conlan, though leader of this mission, had chosen himself for this part of it. He clipped open the cover on his aug and plugged into it his multipurpose optic cable, then found the relevant port in the console and plugged the other end into that. Passive scanning of the vessel's systems quickly revealed the various security systems. All communications were being monitored by sophisticated voice language-recognition programs which passed com up through various layers of filtering, then informed the AI should they hear some sequence to cause concern. A blueprint of the mission plan was also stored, so comparisons could be made and any large deviations equally passed on. There were many other security measures. Conlan noted one flashing a warning to his console—apparently he and the copilot needed to link in the monitoring hardware of their spacesuits. Conlan scanned all these then went in search of the truly important level of security: the one that informed the AI if any of the other systems were being interfered with. He found it stretching weblike across all the other systems. But there was nothing he could do about it at the programming level. His aug might be a sophisticated tool, but he did not yet possess sufficient skill to create the destructive viruses he might need. However, it was possible for him to scan and analyse the ship's hardware.

After a quarter of an hour, Conlan unstrapped himself and moved into the rear of the ship, and stepping over the copilot, he made his selection from the racked tools there. He then pulled up a floor plate and cut through certain optic cables, before returning to his seat, opening the control console, plugging his aug back in, then continuing his selective destruction of the ship's safety and security protocols, beginning with that one concerning suit monitoring for himself and the copilot. When finished he gained complete control of the vessel, and would retain it unless the AI managed to take him out. He offlined autopilot, took hold of his grabship's joystick and pushed it forwards to its limit. Now he changed com to a nonstandard frequency, encoding the signal through his aug.

"Conlan here. What's your status, Braben?"

"Our shuttle is about to dock. We encountered a few problems. One of them is now sitting in the toilet with a broken neck, the rest were minor and put down to glitches associated with the runcible test and the subsequent return of about five hundred technicians."

"You are running twenty minutes late. Why is that?" So asking, Conlan eased off on the joystick. Braben and the rest of the Separatists should have penetrated the runcible's infrastructure by now, causing distracting mayhem.

"Two shuttles got priority ahead of us—probably due to the same glitches and confusion that made things easier for us."

"Okay." Conlan felt a sudden sweat break out over his body. Had their plans been uncovered? He could not see how. "Continue to plan. I'll delay my strike by twenty minutes, but no longer. When you have things under control, you'll have to knock out docking security so I can come in. Best of luck. Out."

Now the runcible lay clearly visible ahead of him. He magnified the view in the forward screen, initiated a grid and selected the unit housing the runcible AI. He knew that unit mounted laser meteor defences and was heavily armoured. Those lasers were also powerful enough to knock out most conventional missiles, and could easily cripple a ship like this one. Certainly the AI would fire on the missile he intended to use.

It made no difference.

Five of them came through the airlock, heavily armoured and opening up with projectile weapons. Security drones dropped from the ceiling and lasers snap-cracked through the air. Two drones exploded, scattering debris about the embarkation lounge. One of the men went down screaming with smoke pouring from his armour's joints, concentrated laser-fire having penetrated his suit. Cams kept going out, and Jebel's perspective kept on changing. Then the last cam was gone, and the images, transferred by Jebel's aug to his visual cortex, blinked out. However, he could still hear the shooting and occasional explosion.

The AIs made no objection to Jebel and his Avalonians roughly tracking the progress of the Prador dreadnought that had destroyed *Avalon Station* and was directly responsible for the death of Cirrella. His unit became one of the best at putting up a ferocious defence against Prador first-strike ground forces. Unfortunately, after grinding that initial assault to a standstill it was usually the first unit to be moved on to the next world or next station, which sometimes put them ahead of the ship—as at Grant's World—but more often behind it when its initial bombardment ended and the ground forces moved in. The AIs understood his vendetta against the Prador aboard that ship to be a powerful motivation indeed. And this time they had placed him on the right world at the right time, where some opportunity, no matter how small, might present itself.

He considered the growing military encampment on the planet below. Forces here were small—about a thousand four-man Sparkind units, numerous war drones, and about fifty thousand ground troops—since most of the runcibles were being employed for evacuation, and Trajeen already accepted as a lost cause, especially now that they knew another ship of the same kind had joined *his* ship. However, that did not mean there should be no resistance at all. The forces here were to give the Prador a bloody nose before retreating, to delay things long enough for a big Polity dreadnought to engage, and to give the new ships steadily being turned out by the shipyards time to deploy around the next world.

But now this: being called up here to deal with this. At first it seemed like a welcome escape from the media attention on the planet below, but Jebel, coldly angry at the best of times and further enraged by events at Grant's World, felt his anger reach new heights upon learning what the first part of his job here entailed.

"Urbanus, is the shuttle away?" he asked over his comlink.

"It is."

"Are they safe?"

"The pilot is okay, but she just found her navigator in the toilet. Dead. Broken neck," the Golem replied.

"They will fucking pay for that."

"I have just received reports from the surface," the runcible AI, for some reason known as George, interrupted, "the technicians whose identity they assumed, were not in fact killed. Someone simply altered their departure times so they just did not turn up at the spaceport."

Jebel mulled that one over. "That's worrying. Again we're seeing some sophisticated planning and computer subversion here."

The attack was well-planned; the Separatists managed to smuggle equipment aboard the shuttle, and their subsequent entry into the complex surrounding this cargo runcible demonstrated that they had obtained information on the positioning of the security drones and cams. It would have succeeded too, but for one of the Separatists on the planet below deciding, at the last moment, that fighting on the side of aliens that blithely destroyed worlds and ate people, might not be such a great idea after all.

The smell of burning wafted through the air, and smoke became visible just below the corridor ceiling. Jebel pushed himself away from the wall and closed his visor. Behind him, twelve other Avalonians, crouched against the wall, did the same. It occurred to him, in that moment, that although having been involved in some hideous conflicts, he had killed only one human being—a man, one firing a pulse rifle into a crowd after having been driven insane by a duff aug, and that was twenty years ago. But he did not think that would be much of a problem in this case. The idea of capturing some of these bastards to interrogate them about their organization was soon abandoned—an exercise about as pointless as obtaining information about underground movements in Dresden just before the bombers arrived. He took a small remote control from his pocket and peered around the corner.

Three armoured Separatists entered ahead of the main group assigned to this corridor. Two other such groups would now be entering the two other main corridors leading from embarkation, and encountering a similar reception. Jebel held up three fingers to those behind him, then crooked a finger. The three nearly reached the corner where Jebel awaited, before the main group of eight entered the corridor behind. Jebel sent the signal and ducked back.

The explosions, multiple, one upon another, lasted for a few seconds. Jebel drew his thin-gun—disdaining anything heavier for this chore. Human wreckage filled the corridor, some of it beginning to scream, the rest mangled and still, and Jebel was reminded of another place and time. The fragmentation mines had torn out the walls. Directly ahead of him, the first of the armoured Separatists tried to push himself upright while turning to gaze at the devastation. In passing, Jebel slapped him on the back. The man turned, raising his seeker-gun, but the ignition delay of the small gecko mine on his armour ran out. The mine thumped, the man belching blood and other substances inside his visor before dropping like a puppet unstrung. The other Avalonians now advanced. Another of the Separatists struggled up onto his knees. An Avalonian put a mine on him before he fully rose, and blew the back out of his helmet. One of the other Avalonians placed a mine on the third, maybe unnecessarily. They moved on towards embarkation. Something bloody whined and scrabbled at the floor as Jebel stepped over it. He identified a head and put one pulse from his thin-gun through it. The whining stopped.

"Have we got them all?" Jebel asked over com.

"Seems like," Urbanus replied. "By the way, Lindy has taken their commander prisoner."

"Why did she do that?"

"I thought I'd better wait for your input, Jebel," Lindy interrupted over com. She sounded a little shaky to him, but then she had probably never killed a human before. "We caught him out… oh, there you are."

Embarkation lay in ruins, unsurprisingly. Jebel's Avalonians were now checking the area. One of the Separatists was down on his knees with his hands interlaced on top of his head, the Avalonian behind him grinding the snout of a laser carbine into the back of his neck. Lindy stood to one side looking a little sick. Urbanus stood before the prisoner. Jebel walked over.

"How did he survive?" he asked.

Urbanus glanced round. "Commanding from the rear. He wasn't in the corridor when we blew the mines. Touch of concussion from the tail end of the blast."

Blood running between his teeth, the man glared up at him. "Do you think you've won?"

Jebel glanced about himself. "Seems pretty decisive to me."

"You'll know… soon enough."

Jebel flung up his hands. "There now, you've gone and done it. Now I'll have to find out what you know, and fast. Y'know, there is a war on."

"You can't—"

Jebel shot him through the kneecap. "Now, perhaps you'd like to explain yourself?"

The larger part of the Trajeen System Cargo Runcible AI observed the scene in the embarkation area, just as it observed many other scenes throughout the runcible installations here and around Boh. Its connection at present with its other part—a submind called George occupying a human skull—presently stood offline while the ship ferrying George and Moria made a short U-space jump back towards Trajeen. It considered intervening in Jebel Krong's interrogation—the man seemed unstable and might kill his prisoner—but his methods thus far were the most effective in the circumstances. And certainly, something else was up.

Their plan to take control of the runcibles so as to hand them over to the Prador when they arrived, could have succeeded only so far, because the AI controlled everything within the complex. Perhaps they had thought to take hostages; no, they must know that the AI would only allow a hostage situation to continue until the Prador ship drew close enough. Then, imbalances in the runcible—a resonance with buffers offline—resulting in no runcible at either end for the Prador to seize. This then must have been only part of their attack. The informational sophistication they had used made that evident.

Grabship?

The AI focused its sensors on the grabship hurtling down under full acceleration. Trying to link to that vessel it found no connection at all. This then, must be the other part of the plan. Did the pilot of that ship intend to ram it into the accommodation unit containing the AI itself? Such suicide missions were not uncommon amid such fanatics.

The AI brought its meteor lasers online and up to power, targeting the approaching vessel, but the ship dropped its load and began to curve away. The AI targeted the load now heading directly towards it. Only seconds away. The AI instantly identified the object, and understood, and admired, the brilliance of the plan: the charge the buffer section contained could not be destroyed or diverted, not with meteor lasers. A brief calculation rendered the result that the AI's chances of survival were minimally better if it did fire upon the buffer. Minimally. In the microseconds remaining, the AI's thoughts went off at a tangent instigated by the nature of this attack, and it realised a probable solution to the problem posed by the approaching Prador dreadnoughts. Too late. It fired the lasers and kept on firing. Most of the energy reflected away from the metallo-ceramic layers armouring the huge store of power inside. Ion trail—so some penetration. Information package to human submind, and into complex computer systems. Intense fusion fire—

The runcible buffer section struck home.

Conlan observed the explosion and smiled. The AI had fired on the buffer section, but even if it had not, the result would have been the same. Its chances of fully rupturing the section with meteor lasers were minimal in the time allowable, but certainly the section would rupture on impact. A plasma fire radiated out into space. The initial EM pulse from all that energy discharging scrambled the AI, and the subsequent fire now fried it. It was dead.

A perfectly executed hit.

Conlan began decelerating the grabship, turning it back towards the runcible.

"Braben, report."

Silence.

"Braben?"

"Braben is otherwise occupied. Who the fuck is this?"

That was not Braben or any voice he recognised—someone else was using Braben's comlink. Conlan felt the knowledge drive into his gut like a blunt drill. Obviously the assault on the complex had failed. If he went there he would be captured, and ECS were not noted for their mercy. He would have to try landing on the planet.

"Oh, brilliant," the other abruptly said. "You know, you turd, in lieu of meeting you myself, I just wish I could see you meet your allies."

Conlan's instinct was to break contact, but his curiosity stirred. "I am not sure I entirely catch your drift."

"Well, obviously you're the fuckwit aboard that grabship who just murdered an AI."

Automatically Conlan replied, "You cannot murder machines."

Now that they knew he was aboard this ship, landing on the planet was also out of the question, for they would track him down to the surface and ECS troops would be waiting for him the moment he stepped out. Only one other option remained: try heading out-system on an intercept course with the approaching Prador ships. But supposing there were enough supplies aboard for him to survive the journey, what would be the reaction of those Separatist allies? He might have killed the AI, but he certainly had not secured the runcible. Always central to Separatist plans lay the idea of them holding this huge bargaining chip. Conlan had seen the newsnet broadcasts. He suspected the Prador might be less inclined to mercy than ECS. A sudden tiredness suffused him as he observed all avenues closing to him.

"To whom am I speaking?" Conlan enquired.

"Oh, let's get on a friendly first-name basis. My name's U-cap, what's yours?"

"I'm Conlan and you know, U-cap, we *will* be meeting very shortly." Conlan thrust the joystick fully forwards and aimed the grabship towards those runcible buffers already in place. If he hit hard and fast enough the chain reaction should be spectacular. Better to go out that way than in some ECS cell or in pieces in some alien gut.

"I don't think so, shit-head."

Conlan did not recognise that voice either, and only belatedly realised it came from behind him. He turned just in time to see his copilot, Anna Vasco, her face masked with blood, and then the heavy handle of a multidriver slammed down onto the side of his head and knocked him into a dark place.

The *Occam Razor* surfaced from U-space and hurtled towards the planetary system. Massive capacitors and laminar batteries stacked up power from fusion reactors, enormous weapons carousels began powering up, replacement parts stood ready in robotic hands for lasers and masers, and the entire internal structure of the ship began to reconfigure for battle.

"I require weapons authorization from my human captain," Occam stated through their link.

The evident irony of this request made Captain Tomalon wonder just how necessary his permission might be. The closer he grew to the AI the more he realised how utterly entangled they were becoming. He granted authorization without even reviewing the sensor data upon which it was based. Inside the great ship he observed those carousels now turning to present missiles to the breech sections of rail-guns, and weapons platforms and turrets rising on titanic rams towards the hull. An exterior view showed him turrets extruding from the ship like the spikes from a mace, rail-gun ports and the business ends of beam weapons opening and one platform for informational warfare finally surfacing. This ship carried appalling destructive capability: besides the beam weapons and rail-guns it also carried missiles containing contra-terrene devices—CTDs—antimatter weapons with a ridiculously high yield. But would it be enough? The Prador ships had already demonstrated that they could take most of what ECS could throw at them and repay it tenfold. He now reviewed the sensor data.

"Where the hell is this?" he asked out loud.

Occam made no reply. Tomalon checked back through the navigational log, found it to be in order, then made comparisons between recorded data on their destination system and this one. They were the same.

"Oh Christ, that's Grant's World."

Through the *Occam Razor*'s sensors he studied the devastated planet. At present it held a kind of temperature stasis: the heat from the weapons employed down there, and the subsequent volcanic activity, were countering the effects of the dust in the atmosphere blotting out the sun. This could not last of course. Within a decade, Grant's World would drop into a centuries-long winter, during which some species might survive to rebuild a living world, as had always been the case on Earth after each catastrophic mass extinction. But this was no misfortune of nature or orbital mechanics. An intelligent species had done this to wipe out members of another intelligent species, in just one battle in an ever-expanding war.

"There are people alive down there," Occam informed him.

"You're kidding."

The temporary stability of the temperature did not mean things were okay on the surface. Hurricane-force winds were swiftly spreading radioactives everywhere, tornadoes drilled across landscapes churning up topsoil and hurling it high. The chances of escaping a tsunami if you were anywhere within a hundred kilometres of a shore, were nil. And if that was not quite enough, the massive quakes released billions of tons of CO_2 from ocean depths whilst the spew from the volcanoes acidified the sky. The atmosphere was no longer breathable for a human being, not even for one breath, unless you wanted to etch out the inside of your lungs.

"I am detecting emergency beacons, but also some com between military units. However, that will have to wait. Let me direct your attention to the objects in nearby space."

Tomalon dragged his attention away from the holocaust. The objects Occam indicated were three big cylinder-shaped vessels, two dark ships bearing a familiar shape but nowhere near the size of the dreadnoughts they sought, and various smaller ships.

Prador.

"Do you need any further weapons permissions?" he asked in their silent communication.

"No. Shall we dance?"

He and Occam drew closer in informational no-space so that Tomalon could not quite say where he ended and the *Occam Razor*'s AI began. Was it he who cut the decelerating burn so they came upon those enemy ships, travelling at over a million kph? Did he fire the rail-guns, launching a swarm of solid projectiles out ahead of them? He was both observer and main participant. For a while he *was* the

Occam Razor.

The rail-gun projectiles slammed into the enemy ships first, puncturing hulls and containment, breaching reactors and occasionally detonating weapons. Two shuttles simply exploded. One of the cylindrical vessels—a troop carrier, Tomalon realised—belched atmosphere through numerous breaches. Next missiles, launched at lower speed then igniting their own drives out from the *Razor*, punched home. They struck perfectly central on two of the carriers, which broke in half trailing atmosphere and fire, while other spillages gave the impression of seed pods snapped open. A close view of those seeds showed thousands of Prador second-children pouring into space with their legs clamped up close to their under-carapaces. Tomalon wondered if they were dead or if they could actually survive in vacuum for a while. He would not have been surprised.

"What the fuck?"

Pain racked Tomalon. Someone was pointing a blow-torch flame at his skin. Exterior view of the *Occam Razor:* turquoise flashes as a phenomenally powerful particle beam sliced a trench through the hull, fire exploding into the spaces inside. Occam immediately redirected missiles aimed for the last troop carrier, zoning them in on the Prador destroyers which remained seemingly untouched by the rail-gun projectiles. The beam struck again. This time from the second destroyer. A weapons turret exploded, rolling fire around the hull. Then the missiles reached their targets.

A full-on hit with a CTD sent one of the destroyers tumbling through space, a huge chunk torn out of it and fires burning inside, but Tomalon was troubled to see that the vessel had survived at all, and now seemed to be trying to right itself. He, or Occam, hit the exposed interior with laser blasts, gutting it until it became still. Those other vessels surviving the initial assault also began to fire on the

Occam Razor. Beam strikes made Tomalon feel warm and caused itches he could not scratch, but there were no more of those ridiculously powerful particle beam strikes. Why? He did not know.

Missiles swarmed out, but the *Occam Razor* outran them. In a hard decelerating burn it swung around Grant's World, its superstructure groaning, and error reports flashing up to the captain's vision from the distant reaches of the ship where repair robots were rushing to breaches like ants to holes in their nest. Coming back towards the remaining Prador ships he detected U-space signatures as some of the Prador ran. However, the remaining destroyer began to accelerate towards them.

Both ships launched solid rail-gun projectiles and explosive missiles. Occam fired two CTDs to detonate in and punch a hole through an approaching swarm of the solid projectiles and followed them with a line of five CTDs running one behind the other. Three closely spaced detonations followed. Briefly, turquoise fire licked over the *Occam*'s hull, then the remaining two weapons hammered home. The Prador ship hurtled out of the ensuing blasts, misshapen, with splits in its hull. Small seeker missiles then, buzzing around the out-of-control ship like horse flies zoning in for an opportunity to bite. They found the splits and detonated inside. The subsequent explosions must have killed everything within, but unnervingly, they did not break the hull, but pushed it almost back into its original shape.

"*Tough fuckers, aren't they?*" Tomalon observed, wincing.

Two further missiles departed the launch tubes, one heading towards the hulk now falling past them, one heading out to find the remains of the other destroyer: beacons—so they could be retrieved for study. ECS had obtained few remains of such ships.

Now they came upon the remaining Prador ships. Launch after launch spread obliteration. The remaining intact troop carrier ceased to be intact. Smaller ships detonated like fire crackers. Lasers, running on subprograms, sought out anything crab-shaped, and seared holes through it. When the *Occam Razor* finally turned and headed back towards Grant's World, very little remained behind it but glowing wreckage and fire.

"*Now the survivors,*" said Tomalon, only slightly troubled by his part in a conflict with quarter neither offered nor requested. As more and more reports filtered out to him, he realised that this conflict was fast becoming total war, and atrocity merely another weapon—employed by both sides.

"*That is not our mission.*"

Chewing on his lower lip, Tomalon disconnected slightly, raised his nictitating membranes and once again saw the interior of the bridge. His mission to pursue, delay, and if possible stop the two Prador dreadnoughts, took precedence. But he did not like the idea of leaving survivors down there.

"Open com to them," he instructed out loud, closing down the membranes on his eyes again. When Occam complied, Tomalon said, "This is Captain Tomalon of the ECS dreadnought the *Occam Razor*. Please send status reports detailing available supplies and the condition of your wounded, and append prior reports and present known casualty figures." Within his close connection with Occam, Tomalon counted fifteen distinct communications and viewed the facts the AI winnowed out. There were a hundred and forty-three survivors. Twelve would die if they did not receive aid within an hour and another fifty-six were stretcher cases that could last maybe another day. All either had sufficient air supplies or were managing with envirosuit filters and purification plants. One group of the fifteen needed assistance because they were located in a highly radioactive area. If they were not out of that area within three hours their dosage levels would kill them despite later rescue.

"It is not just those on the planet," Occam observed.

Communications began arriving from ships scattered throughout the system: people trapped behind bulkheads, engines burnt out, atmosphere venting, leaking reactors... but not many wounded needing medical attention, vacuum being an unforgiving environment.

Through Occam, Tomalon surveyed the holds of the *Occam Razor*. He observed a vast hall with shuttles lining one side like upright soldiers, gleaming and oiled. He observed racking systems containing landing craft and conveyers to take them to their bays.

"Just me and you aboard, so we have no need for all this. They contain medical equipment and supplies."

"Other ECS ships are on their way, certainly, but the plan would fail in one respect: we would need to remain here to guide these craft to their destinations throughout the system and down on the planet. In nearly every case the craft would face problems their programming might not be able to overcome: wrecked vessels, auto-defences still online, storms and EM interference."

"We can't just leave those poor bastards!"

"We will—our solution approaches."

Long range sensors picked out the ECS destroyer moving out from an asteroid field. Its fusion drive was burning dirty, but it was making progress.

"Who is this?" Occam asked over U-com

"Aureus," replied the AI within the destroyer.

"Your crew?"

"All dead."

Through exterior cams Tomalon observed hold doors irising open in the *Razor*'s hull to release a stream of shuttles and landers. Inside, the shuttles were moving down their hall like bullets in a magazine, and the landers were being conveyed—all the massive machinery inside the *Occam Razor* in smooth titanic motion.

"I have given Aureus the control codes for all these vessels," Occam explained. *"Once they are all launched we must leave."*

Tomalon concurred—the human component throwing the final switch allowing the AI to do what it would. When finally the *Occam Razor* turned away from Grant's World, its captain viewed the final estimated casualty figures. One and a half million humans and AIs had died here. His hands clenched into fists, Tomalon began reviewing the big ship's weapons manifests.

6.

How charmingly sweet you sing–

Vagule's tardiness in answering the summons would have been unsurprising in, for example, a human, but as a first-child Prador he should have obeyed instantly—Immanence's pheromonal control over him brooking no delay. Via an additional control unit the captain recently connected into his own nervous system and shell-welded to his carapace—now taking the risk of bypassing his chouds—he linked to the ship's systems and tracked down the errant child. Vagule again experimented on the last four humans allowed him, and was working frenetically to isolate the reasons for them dying. One of the humans however remained alive. Through this fact Immanence supposed the first-child managed to mentally circumvent the summons, knowing precisely its reason. Having failed to obtain positive results with the installation of thrall units, Vagule faced punishment. He managed to disobey the summons by twisting it to not apply while this last human still lived. This might mean Immanence's pheromonal emissions might be waning. He would have to check, and if necessary make the required … adjustments. He ground his mandibles in the nearest a Prador could get to a grin, and swung towards the doors, ordering them to open.

Gnores and XF-326 entered, ahead of a crowd of second-children, which swiftly spread out around the chamber. The first two, however, remained before Immanence.

"Gnores, I will also require a cold cylinder for organ storage," Immanence said.

Gnores relayed that order to one of the second-children, which scuttled off immediately. Immanence now turned his attention to the greatly enlarged second-child beside Gnores.

"XF-326, you will henceforth be known as Scrabbler." Immanence eyed the child, noting that the yellows and purples of its shell were not yet distinct from each other, and that its scent did not yet contain the hormones of adolescence—that period in a Prador's life when it began growing sexual organs underneath a carapace plate at its rear—a plate that in the transition to adulthood it would shed, along with its two back legs, to expose those organs. Sexual activity at this stage remained zero, only to be activated by the absence of a father's pheromonal control. Scrabbler was not yet a first-child, but would be by the time they reached Trajeen.

Gnores swung round to observe Scrabbler for a moment, and Immanence could guess the first-child's thoughts. Gnores saw himself in the position Vagule now occupied, but only briefly, for arrogance and a deluded belief in his own immortality would soon reassert. Thus it was with all Prador first-children when they first felt obstacles to them becoming a Prime falling aside. How long this lasted depended on the Prador concerned. In Vagule it had not lasted very long at all, which was why Immanence intended to be rid of him. Swift perception of the realities bespoke a worryingly dangerous intelligence in a first-child. Immanence did not need them to be too bright, for he did most of their thinking for them.

"Gnores ... the other equipment is being brought up?"

"It is, Father. Second-children will bring it in after him."

Finally, much excitement and skittering around of those second-children still in the corridor announced the approach of Vagule. The first-child dragged himself into the sanctum, Scrabbler and Gnores parting to allow him between them. Vagule scanned each of them, recognising executioners.

"You have failed me, Vagule," said Immanence.

Vagule said nothing—again worrying the captain, for usually the begging and pleading started at this point. The first-child just dipped down lower and rested its claw-tips on the floor.

"But I am not going to kill you."

Vagule perked up suddenly.

That's better.

"In our war against the humans we should not waste resources. And I consider your undeveloped pheromonal glands and cerebral tissue to be valuable resources."

The second-children in the corridor, scrabbling over each other in complete uproar, wheeled the surgical robot into view, then into the chamber. They were obviously experiencing some difficulty with the other larger and heavier object, for there came a rumbling sound, and some loud crunches followed by a couple of squeals and whimpers. Eventually, however, they rolled a large sphere of exotic metal into the sanctum, then cracked open the lid to expose contained grav-motors, steering thrusters, weapons systems, and the central cryo-chamber and attachment equipment.

Emitting a low hissing since seeing the surgical robot, upon seeing this other object Vagule began to squeal.

"Drone shell … no … please?" he managed.

"Step towards me," Immanence ordered.

Vagule turned from side to side, his body quivering and legs dancing a tattoo on the floor. He tried to disobey, but his father's pheromones were strong in this chamber and he could not. He stepped forwards, crouching low before Immanence. The captain reached out with his single large claw, gripped one of Vagule's claws at its base, and twisted it off. Green blood jetted and Vagule shrieked and tried to back away.

"Remain where you are!" Immanence tossed the claw over Gnores and Scrabbler to the second-children, who began fighting over it, then he took hold of the other claw and ripped that off too, sending it after the first. "Strip him now."

Gnores, Scrabbler and those second-children not fighting over the claws, swiftly closed in. Vagule tried to defend himself, but without claws he could not. The crowd swarmed over him, so for a little while he lay buried under a seething mass of his kin. Torn off limbs began to surface in the mass, rapidly broken apart like bait dropped into a shoal of fish. One second-child darted away into the corridor clutching an entire leg, three kin in hot pursuit. Vagule's shrieks slowly petered out, turning to rasping sucking sounds of exhausted agony. When the crowd finally withdrew, only his main body remained, missing all its limbs and even its mandibles.

"Continue," Immanence instructed.

Gnores inserted himself in the hollow back of the surgical robot, sliding his limbs into the pit controls, claws into the slots controlling two spreads of precision limbs and visual turret into the scope interface. After a moment the robot rose on a grav-motor and slid over to Vagule. The procedure thereafter became much more refined and precise than the previous chaos. Using a limb ending in a high-speed circular saw, Gnores cut around Vagule's visual turret, sliced through shell beyond it in a web pattern. With other limbs ending in flat-faced pincers he levered out shell sections with sucking crunches and stacked them to one side, exposing the packed squirmy mass of organs and internal musculature. During a short surgical procedure he removed two whitish pink nodules from either side of Vagule's mouth. These went into the recently arrived cold cylinder. Later, Immanence would have them transplanted into himself: fresh pheromone-producing organs—when they attained their full growth—of tissue that only required small adjustments not to be rejected by his own body.

Gnores hooked out thick optic nerves and tracked them back from the visual turret, which now flopped loose. The pulsing and throbbing within the carapace showed Vagule to be still alive, and he would still be consciously viewing and feeling all this—unconsciousness being a luxury denied to Prador. The optic nerves all linked together and inflated into Vagule's major ganglion, his brain. Gnores hooked up and tracked other nerve trunks away from this and severed them where they branched. Finally he excised the whole mess, cutting the optic nerves close inside the turret at the last. Using nearly all of the surgeon's manipulators he picked up the ganglion and spread out all the nerve trunks in a particular pattern, before turning the lot towards the drone shell. The major ganglion slotted neatly into the central cryo-chamber and, one by one he fed the nerve trunks into the surrounding spread of cryo-tubes to their sockets. With the last one slotted into place, he withdrew. The chamber closed and cold fog began to rise from it as it withdrew deeper into the shell, components rearranged themselves inside and, after a moment, the lid slammed shut.

Immanence clattered his mandibles as if applauding. He knew that right now the processes of cerebral connection and flash-freezing were taking place. In a minute or so base programming would initiate, and then Vagule would obey absolutely without the need for pheromonal control. At the last, movement within Vagule's own carapace finally ceased as his body expired.

"Bring me some of that," Immanence ordered.

Scrabbler leant over the carapace and snipped out the organ that served the purpose of a liver in the Prador and held it up to his father. As Immanence crunched and chewed his way through the delicacy, all around his children grew still, watching him. Upon swallowing the last mouthful, he magnanimously waved his claw.

"Enjoy."

A riot ensued. By the end of it the carapace rested up against one wall, completely scraped clean, and all the limbs lay broken open with the meat winnowed out. Ship lice began venturing from their crevices to snatch up stray gobbets, and Prador burps puttered in the air. Then the spherical drone shell abruptly powered up, lights flicking on and off within various pits in its surface: the barrels of rail-guns extruding momentarily, missile hatches opening and closing. It righted itself, then with a low humming rose from the floor and spun to face Immanence.

"Take your position in the drone cache along with the others and await orders," the captain told it.

It swung round, second-children scattering from its path, floated across the sanctum and into the corridor, turned and motored out of sight.

Most satisfactory.

"You have two hundred humans with which to improve on Vagule's results," Immanence told Gnores. "Be on your way."

Gnores moved off with assertive eagerness.

That would soon change.

Short jumping within a planetary system was not exactly the healthiest of occupations, since the presence of massive bodies, like suns, tended to over-complicate the vectors and result in the ship concerned being forced from U-space in very small pieces. This was why most spaceships surfaced a safe distance from any gravity well and approached their destination under conventional drives. Besides sheer convenience, this was why the runcible superseded ships for transportation within the Polity. Also, the resulting lack of ships within the Polity prevented ECS from mounting a creditable defence against the Prador. Strapped into her acceleration chair—for the ride might be bumpy during this short jump—Moria considered that for a moment. Huge shipyards, currently under construction, were racing to rectify that lack, and she reckoned that should the Polity survive this conflict, such a lack would never again be allowed. This probably meant death to the cargo runcible idea. She unstrapped herself.

The weird sensation of something twisting out of kilter finally passed. The vessel surfaced into the real, intact. She relaxed for a moment, considering the quandary of runcibles and ships. Though for the latter surfacing near gravity wells held dangers, the former were often positioned on planets—right in those wells. It all devolved down to the fast calculations required at the interface, the surfacing point, and to modelling. With a fixed runcible on the surface of a planet, the AI held in its mind a model of the surrounding system—all the space-time maps including those venturing beyond the event horizon of the warp—so it did not need to calculate those. Also an AI lay at each end, making the connection. The nearest analogy she could think of was to ocean travel between two islands. The spaceships were like old-fashioned submarines that needed to surface to see where they were going so they could motor into port without smashing into something. The runcible, however, was a transit tube laid along the ocean bed and whatever used it, be that humans or cargo, could not deviate from its course—entry and exit points were nailed down. Perhaps that was it! Perhaps the problem with the recent test related to drift in the spatial positions of the cargo runcibles! That the tube mouths were not sufficiently nailed down?

"George?" she turned towards him. "Could it be simply spatial drift?" As she said it she winced, realising the AI would have calculated for that and the solution to the problem could not be anything so simple.

No reply from George, however. He remained utterly still, eyes open and staring at the ceiling, still strapped into his seat. Drool ran down his chin.

"George?"

A slight flick of the eyes. Slowly he raised his hand and wiped the back of it across his mouth. He turned his head slightly, focusing on her.

"One for the mouse, one for the crow, one to rot and one to grow," he said.

"What?"

He gave a puzzled frown, then raised his fingers to his mouth and touched his lips as if they betrayed him. "Fine words butter no parsnips," he decided.

Something was seriously wrong.

"What you don't know can't hurt you." He reached out and tapped her aug.

Moria stayed very still for a moment. Necessarily offline throughout the U-jump, her aug had not reinstated now that this ship travelled through realspace towards the cargo runcible. She tried reconnection and there came almost a hesitation, then, via a server on the runcible, she routed into the chaotic Trajeen network. Fragments of news stories reached her first, but she kept getting knocked out of the network and receiving all sorts of strange error messages. Something bad was happening: Separatists … an explosion. Then:

EDDRESS REQUEST >

OFFLINE EDDRESS REQUEST?

ACCEPT?

Moria began to review the information attached to the eddress request, but just stopped at the name:

JEBEL KRONG.

What the hell is he doing here? But then she immediately answered her own question. She knew about Jebel Krong and his Avalonians: stories about him were much relished by the newsnet services, since they were part of the small amount of good news coming from the front. He was here because the Prador were coming. But why did he want to communicate with her? Only one way to find out. She gave permission for her eddress to be used—activating voice and image com.

"Moria Salem," stated the requester.

"Well, I'm pleased to make your acquaintance, Jebel Krong, but why are you talking to me?"

The connection hardened now—she rather suspected military com software to be involved—and his image appeared in her visual cortex. She took in the chameleon-cloth fatigues with their black webbing, the famous crab buttons, and the austere face with his V-shaped scar.

"Big hole in the networks at the present, so I rather suspect you don't have the full story. That hole was once occupied by the one known as George."

"What?"

Moria blinked, looked at her companion—the image of Jebel still retained.

George said, "What's done cannot be undone," and she understood him.

"My god, what happened?"

"Separatists attacked here, and though they did not manage to take control, they did manage to murder the AI."

"But I still don't understand why you have contacted me. Is it because of George here?"

"I beg your pardon?"

"Some confusion, I think. The Trajeen Cargo Runcible AI has a submind … an avatar. Part of its mind resides in a vat-grown human body presently sitting beside me spouting proverbs."

"I see … no, I am not contacting you because of that, though that particular George may be of some use to you. I am contacting you because you are now apparently in charge of the cargo runcible project. In the instants before it was destroyed the AI ordered this. I'm not sure I entirely understand the reasons why, since I have just received orders that both runcibles must be destroyed to prevent the Prador getting hold of them."

"Oh, fuck-shit!"

"Yes, most apposite. We'll discuss the situation further after you dock. Out."

The connection broke and Moria once again turned to George. No proverbs were forthcoming. He merely blinked, held his hand up before his face and wiggled his fingers, his expression slightly puzzled as if never having seen these digits before.

The two Prador vessels caused sufficient disturbance in U-space for Occam to easily follow them, though the term "follow" in a continuum without physical dimension or time strained to breaking point. Tomalon checked realspace maps of the sector and studied the two predicted targets in their path: a transfer station orbiting a red dwarf—one of those places required to control runcible traffic so millions would not arrive at one destination all at once, but now being used to supply ships near the line—and the Trajeen system. He accessed information on the latter and felt his stomach clenching. The human population there stood close to a billion. All sorts of stations and bases were scattered throughout the system, which itself contained two living worlds. Yet, why were those two ships heading there? Yes, being a heavily populated Polity system Trajeen was a viable target, but on the whole the big ships like these were hitting targets of a strictly military significance. Trajeen did not really fit the pattern.

"*Why there?*" he asked, in his mind.

"*Runcibles,*" Occam replied immediately.

Tomalon already knew they had built and were testing a cargo runcible at Trajeen. But why would the Prador want to seize one of them? A runcible required an AI to operate it and no AI would willingly do so for the Prador. And until now the Prador showed little interest in the devices.

"*Why?*"

"*Because these runcibles, being located out in space, will be much easier to take, especially having been originally taken control of by Prador allies: Separatists.*"

"*What?*"

"*Allow me to acquaint you with the details contained in a recent communication I have received.*" So saying the AI swiftly transferred the information to Tomalon's interface. The data-stream being buffered, so Tomalon did not have to take it in all at once, delayed his understanding for a few seconds, then he got the gist.

"*The bastards ... but I still don't see why. Do the Prador think they can make runcibles work without AIs?*"

"*Not known. Perhaps that is what they told the Separatists. Perhaps they believe so. A more likely scenario is that they are after the support technology, which in itself has many weapons applications.*"

Tomalon did not like some of the ideas that began occurring to him: a runcible gate, even without an AI to control it, could be used to instantly accelerate matter to near-c—just one idea without thinking about it very deeply.

"They must destroy those runcibles," he said out loud.

Out loud as well, using the com system in the bridge, Occam replied, "That is currently in hand. Now we are about to surface near the transfer station where our two Prador friends have just arrived."

"I should give you weapons clearance."

"You already gave it back at Grant's World."

"You don't need it again?"

"Not unless you cancel that clearance. I advise you not to do that."

It was more of a warning than a threat, but not much more.

As they surfaced from U-space, Tomalon closed up with Occam and banished his interior perception of the bridge, becoming one again with the ship and its sensors. They arrived only minutes behind the two Prador ships, and minutes were all it took. A long, glittering cloud of debris lay directly ahead like a scar across vacuum—all that remained of the transfer station. The two ships lay beyond it, gleaming in red light as they accelerated towards the dwarf sun, probably to slingshot round and fling themselves clear before engaging their U-engines again. Still hurtling along at the velocity with which it earlier entered U-space, the *Occam Razor* ignited its fusion engines and accelerated too. Weapons turrets and platforms rose, missiles and solid rail-gun projectiles loaded. Tomalon expected Occam to shoot out a swarm of rail-gun missiles as before, but that procedure abruptly stood down.

"Why not?"

"Further information package received. While controlling the craft we left, Aureus also sent telefactors to study the remains

of the Prador destroyers. The exotic metal armour contains piezoelectric layers and s-con grids linked to what Aureus finally identified as thermal generators. Small strikes merely provide them with more energy with which to strike back.”

“Hence that particle beam they hit us with?”

“Certainly.”

“Our options now?”

“We get, as one Jebel Krong would say, ‘up close and personal.’ We need to hit hard enough to kill them before they can utilize the energy from our strikes.”

The paths of the two Prador vessels now diverged. One swung away from its slingshot route, spun over nose-first towards the *Occam Razor*, and began decelerating.

“Ah, it seems they want to talk,” Occam commented.

Within Tomalon’s perception the view into a Prador captain’s sanctum opened out, revealing the limbless captain floating just above the floor. Tomalon understood, from intelligence gathered during other conflicts, this to be a Prador adult, and that the fully limbed troops ECS more often encountered were the young. It grated its mandibles to make some hissing and bubbling sounds, and the translation came through a moment after.

“So ECS does have some real ships,” it said.

“Would you like to reply?” Occam enquired.

“Why not?” Tomalon sensed the link establishing and spoke out loud, “Who am I addressing?”

“I am Captain Shree—a name you will know but briefly.”

“Well, Shree, we do have real ships and you have sufficiently irritated us that we feel beholden to use them.”

“I look forward to our meeting. It is a shame we cannot meet in the flesh, but alas I have a war to help win and no time to peel that admirable vessel to find you.”

“Fuck me, B-movie dialogue. Why is this character

talking?"

"Perhaps to make him the focus of our attack rather than the other vessel," Occam replied.

"Should we ignore him and go after the other one?"

"I rather think not. If we do we'll have Shree behind us. Upon experience of their destroyers I am not sure if we could survive that particular vice."

"I see that your companion captain is not so anxious to make our acquaintance," Tomalon noted.

"Oh, but Captain Immanence has a rendezvous to keep. He passes on his best regards and looks forward himself to encountering more vessels like your own. Thus far the conflict has become boringly predictable."

The Prador vessel now launched a fusillade of missiles, zipping up in the light of the sun like emergency flares. The *Occam* abruptly swerved and now did launch rail-gun projectiles, but aimed to intercept the missiles rather than hit the Prador ship. On their current trajectory the solid projectiles that did not strike missiles would pass above it, but only just—it would look like a near miss. Within the great ship Tomalon observed some alterations being made: CTD warheads being diverted away from the low-acceleration rail-guns usually used, to one of the more powerful ones. They were being loaded along with the solid projectiles so that every tenth launch would be a CTD.

"Isn't that a little dangerous?" he asked. Such warheads were not often accelerated up to relativistic speeds, since the stress might cause some breach of the antimatter flask they contained. If that happened while the missile accelerated up the gun rails the results might be … messy.

"Not nearly as dangerous as giving this ship time to take us apart," Occam replied. *"The chances are one in twenty of an in-ship detonation."*

Prador missiles began exploding in vacuum as the

projectiles slammed into them. Shree's vessel immediately changed course to intercept any of those projectiles to get through—deliberately putting itself in their path. Occam slow-launched programmed CTD warheads down towards the sun, and ramped up its acceleration towards the enemy. Both vessels came within each other's beam range. A particle beam struck the *Occam Razor*, cutting a boiling trench through hull metal. Tomalon felt this as pain, but this being a facility of which he felt no need, he tracked down its source—a diagnostic feedback program—and cancelled it.

Occam used lasers to hit incoming missiles, intercepted others with hard-fields, then opened up with masers on the Prador ship. It seemed a foolish tactic, in view of what they now knew about that exotic metal armour, but Tomalon understood that Occam did not want Shree to realise how much they knew. The missiles launched down towards the sun, came up with the solar wind—more difficult to detect—and closed on Shree's vessel. The Prador began to hit them with lasers, but some got through and exploded on the exotic metal hull. Huge dents became visible, and one split in which fires glowed, but even as Tomalon saw these, the dents began to push out and the split to close. Now four particle cannons targeted the *Occam Razor*, using the energy these strikes generated. They ripped into the *Razor*'s hull. One of them struck a weak point and exploded through, and Tomalon observed internal beams glowing white hot and ablating away, some massive hard-field generator cut in half, human living quarters scoured with fire that would have incinerated anyone in there.

The two ships were still on a collision course, and Tomalon realised the Prador vessel would not divert—it did not need to. In a seemingly desperate measure the *Occam Razor* turned—taking more particle weapon strikes on fresh hull metal—to use its main fusion engines to change course. The sudden massive acceleration caused huge floor sections and corridors, already weakened, to collapse inside the ship. The ship's internal mechanisms began reconfiguring it, relocating the bridge pod, and moving other more vulnerable ship components deeper inside. A close pass at mere hundreds of kilometres. A beam strike hit the hull and passed straight through the ship, exploding out of the other side.

"Close enough," said Occam coldly, and began firing that rail-gun.

They were unlucky, the one in twenty chance playing against them as the sixth CTD detonated inside the rail-gun. The explosion tore into thousands of tonnes of superstructure and hull, shattered much inside the ship and filled it with a brief inferno. Tomalon clung to the arms of his interface chair as the entire bridge pod flew twenty metres before slamming to a halt against a bulkhead. He thought that was it, they were dead, but still connected into the sensor arrays he watched three antimatter warheads, travelling at a substantial portion of light speed, strike home on the Prador vessel. The triple explosion seemed as one to human perception, but Tomalon slowed it so he could truly see what happened. The first detonation pushed a crater into the ship's hull nearly a quarter of its size, the second ripped through and exploded from the other side to blow out a glowing funnel of the super-tough metal, and the last finished the job—cutting the ship in half.

Tomalon viewed the devastation within the *Occam Razor*. He was glad not to have felt it as pain, because this would have been of the smashed-open ribs and evisceration by fire variety.

"The other ship?" he enquired.

"It has gone," Occam replied.

"Probably thought it pointless to waste weapons on us."

"Probably," Occam agreed.

"What do we do now?"

"There is some damage to those field projectors that protect human passengers during U-space transit. However, our U-space engines are undamaged. It will be necessary for you to be unconscious during the journey, while I make the repairs that I can."

"We're going after it?"

"That is our mission."

The Prador, Tomalon realised, were not going to win this war.

Conlan rose slowly to consciousness, his head throbbing and a foul dryness in his mouth. He found himself lying on cold metal, the feel of a diamond-pattern foot grip against his face. He remained motionless, and keeping his eyes closed listened intently. No one stood nearby. He opened his eyes and tilted his head slightly to obtain a better view of his surroundings: just the floor and metal walls and a ceiling, by the look of them only recently welded into place. His cell. He tried to push himself up to stand and discovered something wrong. They had removed his hand and his artificial arm. Using his other arm only, he completed the task.

The cell stood three metres square with a single bulkhead door set in one wall—no bed, no facilities. Up in one corner protruded a single visible security camera. He walked over to the door and inspected it. No electrical controls and someone had removed the inner manual wheel. Easing himself down next to it, resting his back against the wall, he sat on the floor. His mistake, he realised, was not checking to see if his copilot was dead. Obviously, Heilberg's hand, breaking from its mountings on his arm, softened the blow. Feeling the side of his head he discovered a sore split and blood crusted in his hair. Much blood had also spattered over the shoulder of his flight suit—to be expected from a head wound.

Conlan now used his aug to access the chaotic networks of Trajeen and learnt to his satisfaction that he had achieved his initial aim—the AI was dead, hence the chaos. Little other information became available however, and when his aug dropped offline for the eighth time, he did not bother to reconnect. It would be no help to him now.

"Can anyone hear me?" he called. "I need medical attention, somewhere to wash and a toilet, or is this the usual civilized manner with which ECS treats its prisoners?"

Movement outside now. Locking mechanisms clonked. Conlan heaved himself to his feet and stood close to the door. If he did this just right he might be able to get past whoever came in, maybe relieve them of a weapon in passing. He would have to rely on training and instinct thereafter, which he possessed in plenty. They would not expect him to act this quickly and decisively. The door, he realised, opened on hydraulic rams, so knocking it back into someone's face was no option. When it stood partially open he glimpsed a figure beginning to step through. He kicked hard, towards a torso, but instead of the expected impact, something clamped on his ankle. The figure came through, hauling his leg up trapped between upper arm and chest, forcing him back. He leapt, spinning his other foot off the floor and aimed towards the head. The figure released his trapped leg, ducked under the kick, and a fist like a bag of marbles came up into Conlan's kidneys. Conlan came down on his feet, but unbalanced by his missing arm, staggered. He turned, trying to aim a chop, which was slapped along its path. Then an ECS enviroboot slammed up into his testicles and Conlan abruptly lost the will to fight.

"You're very fast," said a voice, "but I've been in constant combat with those possessing substantially more limbs than you. And the lack of an arm can cause a surprising amount of imbalance—that's something I know well."

Focusing through tears Conlan observed the man standing over him, then further pain roiled through him and he leant over and vomited. It felt as if his balls had been hammered up into his stomach. He coiled into himself on the floor, closed his eyes, and just wished his copilot had hit him a lot harder. Finally, an eternity later, he managed to pull himself into a hunched sitting position and studied his opponent.

"Now, are you ready to talk?"

The man wore chameleon-cloth fatigues striated with black webbing. He didn't look physically boosted or augmented, though he did wear a cerebral aug on the side of his head. His face was thin and acerbic, fair hair close cropped and a distinctive V-shaped scar marred his cheek. Conlan felt he should recognise this individual, but did not. Almost instinctively he loaded the image of the face into his aug and ran a search through the device's memstore, rather than try to connect to the net. He soon obtained the information he sought.

Jebel Krong… why here?

He realised this was the one he spoke to from the grabship, though Krong named himself U-cap then … he remembered: *up close and personal…*

"Now," said Krong, "I want you to tell me, in detail, what was supposed to happen after you took control of this place."

"Go fuck yourself."

The boot slammed into his guts and lifted him off the floor. Before he could even think of recovering, a knee pinned his left arm to the floor, one hand closed on his throat, while the other clamped on his testicles. He shrieked and tried to fight free. *That* hand closed tighter and he felt one of his bruised testicles taken between a forefinger and thumb, and crushed. The world faded away.

Conscious again, wishing he wasn't. Krong squatted down facing him, unarmed. Did he hold Conlan in such contempt?

"Now, I have part of the story from your friend Braben, before he fainted, just like you. I will hurt you very very badly unless you tell me what I want to know. And believe me, please, what I just did to you is nothing. We have medical equipment here that can keep you alive far beyond where you would reasonably expect the relief of dying."

Conlan felt real fear growing in him then. Always, before, he was the one dishing it out rather than receiving it. He knew that he would eventually talk, so what purpose did he serve by remaining silent?

"ECS agents … don't … torture people," he managed.

"Tell me your name," Krong countered.

Conlan considered holding that back, but decided, upon his experience thus far, answering to be a small concession to make. "Conlan."

Krong grimaced. "Conlan, ECS agents usually don't torture people, since the results tend to be of questionable utility. Usually, once guilt is proven, further information is obtained by a mind ream. It's interesting technology similar to that involved in installing an aug. It has to be directed by an AI, and even then not a lot remains of the victim's brain. But as you know, we no longer have an AI here even if we did possess the required equipment. However, ECS agents are trained to quickly extract information when the situation warrants it. They will use specialized drugs or torture. No drugs here, though, and I'm not an ECS agent, I'm a soldier fighting a war against a species who seem intent on wiping out the human race, and my patience is running out." Krong stood. "Do you know what Prador do to some of their captives?"

Conlan shook his head. He felt he could move about now, but kept very still.

Krong continued, "They keep them alive, for as long as possible, while they eat them. I'll use pliers and metal snips on you … to give you an as near to authentic experience as I can manage in the circumstances. What was supposed to happen here!"

The moment this man let his guard down or turned his back, Conlan would rip his throat out. That circumstance seemed unlikely for the present. Conlan told him all.

The three Avalonians who met Moria and George at the airlock were a tough-looking bunch; they were armed and their chameleon-cloth fatigues showed burns and spatters of blood. Stepping out into the embarkation area Moria gazed round at the mess: shattered drones hung from the ceiling on their power cables, energy weapon burns marred the walls and one entire section had been torn out by an explosion.

"Separatists," stated one of the Avalonians, a hard-faced woman who then gestured to the other side of the area with the pulse-rifle she held.

Moria did not require that explanation.

In addition to all the damage in here, Moria saw queues of runcible technicians standing with baggage at their feet by all the other locks. They glanced at her with a fearful lack of curiosity, obviously intent on departing this place.

"This way," said the woman.

With the two other Avalonians behind them and the woman leading, Moria and George walked over to one of the corridors leading into the station. Here the wreckage was even worse with walls torn out, jags of metal protruding, insulation and fried optics hanging free. Some grav-plates were torn up so they necessarily crossed areas where the grav fluctuated disconcertingly. There was blood on the floor, lots of it, but what really turned Moria's stomach was the sight of an armour shoulder-plate with part of the shoulder still inside it. Moria halted, resting one hand against an undamaged section of wall and tried to get her nausea under control. The woman turned impatiently, then her expression softened.

"I know, it's horrible, but we are being forced to make horrible choices," she said.

"When the going gets tough the tough get going," George intoned.

Moria could not help herself, she abruptly burst into laughter, and when she finally got that under control she felt a sudden gratitude towards him. Once out of the corridor she tried to put the image of that shoulder-plate out of her mind, and nearly succeeded by the time they reached their destination and their guards departed.

Jebel Krong and a Golem waited in one of the small lounges overlooking Trajeen, which lay much closer now, as the runcible was being moved back to stable orbit around the planet following the test. Moria recognised the Golem as that constant companion of Krong's: Urbanus. Immediately she asked about the runcible technicians queuing for departure.

"We're evacuating the complex," explained Urbanus. "It seems rather foolish keeping these people here where they make a nice easy target for the Prador. Anyway," he shrugged, "I'm sure they won't want to be around when we blow this place."

Obviously Moria knew all about that, though still she could not help but feel a rebellious anger at the act being so casually mentioned. Glancing at George she discerned no reaction to the words from him. His head just kept swinging from side to side, studying his surroundings as if seeing them for the first time.

Krong turned from gazing out at the view, and gestured to one of the sofas. "Please, take a seat."

"How was the AI destroyed?" Moria asked while she sat.

"One of the Separatists managed to take control of a grabship delivering a runcible buffer section. He dropped the section straight on top of the AI and the massive discharge fried everything."

George, now seated beside Moria, stated, "Providence is always on the side of the big battalions."

Krong stared hard at him for a long moment before replying, "Or the big, well-armoured spaceships that are coming this way." The man then turned away from George dismissively and eyed Moria. "You are only here as a courtesy, and because I am very curious to know why the AI felt the need to put you in charge of this place during the last microseconds of its existence. AIs do not do such things on a whim."

"But I am not in charge, am I?" Moria noted, that shoulder-plate momentarily returning to haunt her.

"Let us say I welcome your input."

"Most helpful," Moria pretend smiled. "Then let me say I too am curious about the AI's motives." Aug com with this man did not give a full impression of him. In the same room with him, she felt a *frisson* of fear. Here stood someone driven, dangerous, she could feel it in the energy that kept him on his feet and see it in his expression—one she could only describe as pitiless. Perhaps recent events were causing her to overreact.

"Do you have any suggestions?" he asked.

The AI's motives were opaque to Moria, only suggestions as to lines of enquiry occurred. "Have you tried the planetary AIs—those running the runcibles on the surface?"

"I have, but they possess little time to spare for me. They're running the runcibles at maximum rate, open-port all across the Polity. They are also organizing planetary defences. Apparently George," he shot a penetrating look at the AI's human representative in the room, "passed on to them no information about your appointment. Perhaps the reasons for it became apparent in those last moments, prior to it making the decision. It could also be that information was lost in the subsequent net collapse."

"Perhaps if I knew more about what happened and what is likely to happen?"

Krong held up a hand, then addressed his companion, "Urbanus, take George with you and try to question him. Use signing, writing—anything you can think of. If necessary, see if you can fit him with an aug and try to access his brain directly. Liaise with one of the planetary AIs; maybe we can come up with something useful."

"If the decision was made in the last moments," Urbanus observed. "George here will probably possess no knowledge of it. I understand he remained out of communication, in a U-jump, when Conlan destroyed the AI."

"Nevertheless he was part of that AI."

Urbanus nodded and stepped forwards to place a hand on George's shoulder.

George stood meekly and said, "The worth of a thing is what it will bring." He followed Urbanus from the room.

"That is both annoying and worryingly close to making sense. I think he might be trying to tell us something," said Krong.

"Proverbs are like that … this … Conlan?"

Krong looked at her piercingly. "Your aug is unusual, I understand?"

"It is."

"So too is Conlan's, but he played for the other team.

He organised an attack up here to seize this place while he himself piloted the grabship. We were forewarned and managed to stop the former but not the latter. We now have Conlan locked in a cell."

That raised all sorts of questions that Moria ran through and discarded as irrelevant. She concentrated on the heart of it: "Why?"

"He worked for the Separatists here who were apparently being financed, indirectly, by the Prador Kingdom. Apparently the Prador promised to destroy all the AIs and put humans back in charge again."

Moria snorted derisively.

"My thoughts too. Once this place came under Separatist control with the AI destroyed, Conlan was to link in, using his aug, to the connection between this runcible and the one at Boh, taking control of all systems there that were once controlled from this end by the AI. It seems he would have been able to prevent reattachment of the units of the complex there by shutting down environmental controls and seizing control of meteor collision lasers. The technicians there would have been fighting to survive and would have had little time to do the runcible any damage before the Prador arrived to take it."

"I see."

"You don't seem surprised."

Moria shook her head. "George was slowly uncovering what it's possible for me to do with such an augmentation. Subversion of computer systems was involved but I can see how it would be possible."

"I had a difficult time accepting it myself but for the sophistication of the attack. I thought he was overestimating his abilities." He grimaced. "He did, though apparently not those ones."

"What's happening now?" she asked.

"Two Prador ships are on their way here so any spatial defence we could mount in the limited time will be... ineffective. We've a vessel already in transit to Boh to pick up the technicians there, and once it is loaded, another will be following, its crew detailed to conceal CTD space mines within that runcible's structure. We are also mining this one. There is a Polity dreadnought called the *Occam Razor* in pursuit of those two ships, but..." Jebel shook his head. "I haven't seen anything we've got manage to stop just one of those bastards."

"So we burn our crops behind us," Moria stated.

"Yes. Intriguing and frustrating though this puzzle concerning your promotion might be, I still have to work on the basis that the best way to stop the Prador seizing these runcibles is to obliterate them. My strongest wish is that the Prador on one particular ship take the Boh runcible aboard before discovering the mines." He gazed out at Trajeen again now.

"Particular ship?" she asked.

He glanced back at her. "One of those is the ship that destroyed *Avalon Station*. The one that set this war in motion and made me the man I now am." Something bitter, perhaps a little insane, flashed across his expression, then he seemed to take it under control as he turned to face her fully again. "Unless the rate of progress of the two ships changes, they should be here within the week."

Moria shivered; he stood with his hands clasped behind his back, Trajeen precisely haloing his head. Two of the moons were visible; Vina, identifiable by its speed of transit, swung over above him like some ominous sign. He seemed a prophet of doom.

"How many will be evacuated from the planet by then?" It never occurred to her to wonder if she would be among them.

"Not even ten per cent," he replied. "I think we're done talking now." He turned back towards the window.

In her aug she received a transmission from him containing all the records of recent events. It was a dismissal.

Vagule's thoughts cycled with frosty precision in his flash-frozen brain. With his spherical armoured body ensconced on one rack in the drone cache, he observed through his sensors eight others of his kind arrayed in similar racks beside him. Communication being possible he listened in to some of the exchanges between the other drones:

"Father will send us into battle soon and we can kill humans."

"I look forward to demonstrating my loyalty to Father."

"Kill the humans and all Father's enemies."

"I have detected a fault in my rail-gun which will make me less able to serve Father."

"Call for maintenance—to not be perfectly maintained is disloyal."

"I have called for maintenance."

And so it went: the continuous affirmation of purpose with discussions straying into the subjects of weaponry, tactics and occasionally into analysis of previous engagements. Vagule, who could do no less than feel utterly loyal to Immanence, also understood that loyalty to be imposed by electronic means just as it was previously imposed by his father's pheromones. His past life lay open to his inspection and he remembered his father's treatment of him with painful clarity. It seemed that though disobedience was no option, his ability to think about his lot was no longer confused by those physical pheromonal effects. However, most of those here were second-children who only vaguely recollected being anything other than war drones. They did not possess an underlying stratum of memory to run counter to their imposed loyalty. There was, however, one other drone here like himself.

"You are the new drone," said that other.

"I am Vagule."

"Yes, a first-child Prime."

"Who are you?"

"I am Pogrom and I too was a first-child Prime, though only your presence here has reminded me of that."

Vagule knew nothing of any first-child called Pogrom and only then did it occur to him that others went through the same experiences before him.

"When were you a first-child?"

"Back on home-world when Immanence still possessed four legs and both claws and before this ship was built. I do not know how long ago, only that thirty first-children have served since then."

Thirty?

Vagule realised hundreds of years must have passed. "What was your infraction?"

"I became too old and Father's pheromones began to have less and less of an effect upon me. He ordered me upon a mission to attack a rival in the King's Council, one from which I was not expected to return. But I completed my mission—I booby-trapped one of the rival's spare control units with diatomic acid which later ate out his insides when he shell-welded the unit to his under-carapace—and returned."

"Then you served Father well." Surprisingly well, since most Prador adults buried themselves behind layer upon layer of defences and were particularly difficult to kill. During the vicious infighting, which was the way Prador conducted their politics, it was the first- and second-children that did the dying and few adults actually ended up dead. They usually only lost or gained wealth or status.

"Yes, I served Father well. Upon my return he called me to him, and it was obvious he intended to strip my limbs and kill me, for already my back limbs were loosening as I made a slow transition to adulthood. I attacked him and managed to tear off one of his legs before the second-children and new first-child Prime-in-waiting managed to tear off all my limbs."

"You attacked Father?"

"I attacked him and am shamed and, as you must know, not shamed."

"I will serve Father," Vagule stated, but beneath that knew he would rather not.

"Father kept me alive for fifty days, feeding small pieces of my organs to the second-children all the while."

"As is just."

"As is just," the other agreed. "At the end of that period, when my death approached, he transferred me to this drone shell. He was much angered because my attack on him necessitated the installation of his first grav-motor, for he could no longer walk unaided."

"You angered Father and were rightly punished," Vagule stated, feeling a core of jealousy for he had not done so much.

"Let us now do weapons inventories, for that is always interesting," said Pogrom.

"Yes, let us do that," Vagule replied, knowing this was as much fun as he was going to have, ever again.

7.

But what shall we do for a ring–

Spying through the many sensory heads positioned in the vast hold, as became his custom, Immanence observed, listened to, and smelt the remaining human prisoners. Very few of them were standing, and most of them situated themselves in a small, close mass on the side away from the sewerage drains. They made themselves as comfortable as possible using clothing stripped from the dead. One human sat at the perimeter clutching a human leg bone which he used to club ship lice that scuttled too close to the female corpse beside him. He obtained this bone some while back from the remains of a man who tried to attack Gnores and was eaten alive in front of his fellows for his efforts.

Now, while the captain watched, another human subdued the one with the bone while two others dragged the female corpse from the crowd to beside one of the drains where later a second-child would come for it. Earlier they all, like the bone wielder, had concealed and protected their dead, obviously suffering some primitive reaction upon guessing the final destination for those corpses: dissection for study, then to be eaten. But obviously someone had taken charge—removing these items before the smell rendered their imprisonment less pleasant than at present.

Well over two hundred died since Gnores took over from

Vagule, but not all of those died as a direct result of the new Prime's experiments. Immanence eyed the numerous reports on autopsies conducted by Scrabbler. Out of the total of seven hundred and sixty prisoners taken aboard, twenty-one died quickly from injuries suffered during capture and a further fifty-three from subsequent infections—mainly from those injuries caused when second-children ripped away their cerebral hardware; two died giving birth—one of the children stillborn and the other dying a day later; three hundred and eighty died as a result of thrall implantation and thirteen killed themselves. That should have left two hundred and ninety-one prisoners, but in the last few days over a hundred of the remainder died.

Scrabbler quickly ascertained the cause as a virulent cross-species disease spreading in the hold, its effects much amplified amid a despairing and much weakened population. It seemed the disease was a viral mutation from something carried by ship lice—who, given the opportunity, fed on both the dead and the living—and it possessed interesting possibilities. Scrabbler was now working on even more deadly strains, and methods of producing them in a sporuler form suitable for dumping in large quantities into the upper atmosphere of a world.

Gnores was now, of course, dragging his many feet, terrified that Immanence might count the disease deaths as part of his allotted two hundred, and knowing that even if the captain did not, he only had twenty test subjects left. Immanence now came to the conclusion that human beings were simply too weak for thrall implantation and that until a stronger form of human could be found the whole project would have to be put on hold. He considered his options.

Within a week they would be arriving at the Trajeen system. Since the unfortunate demise of Shree, he felt he should make his approach somewhat more circumspect than originally intended. Certainly the Polity dreadnought that destroyed the other Prador ship would be no problem, since he very much doubted it would be going anywhere after that last battle, but there might be others about. Laying off just outside the system he would contact those dim human agents who were working for the Kingdom to see if they had, as promised, gained control of the two runcibles. If they confirmed this, he would then approach the Boh runcible sending some of his children ahead to scan the device for anything of sufficient explosive yield to damage his ship, though the hold in which he intended to store the runcible was armoured with the same exotic metal as the hull.

By this time, Immanence hoped to have the problem with thrall implantation solved, with numerous useful humans enslaved and placed throughout the ship. The ninety or so humans left were in the way, and Immanence did not relish the idea of placing them anywhere else in the ship. They might be weak and despairing, but no doubt, given the opportunity, they would try to cause some damage. They had, after all, nothing to lose. Regretfully, the captain came to a decision. He opened one communication channel.

"Scrabbler, take a hundred of your fellows down to the hold, slaughter the remaining humans and move them to the cold store with the rest."

"Yes, Father," that first-child replied enthusiastically.

Now the other channel: "Gnores, report to me in my sanctum, immediately."

"Yes, Father." Gnores' enthusiasm seemed somewhat lacking.

Immanence now called up images from the hold on his bank of hexagonal screens, and routed the sounds and smells into his sanctum rather than directly into his sensorium through a control unit; then he swung round to face the doors and opened them. Gnores arrived somewhat later, not as "immediately" as the captain would have wished, and hesitated at the entrance.

"Enter and stand before me, Gnores."

The first-child Prime stepped inside on quivering legs. He scanned all around inside the sanctum and once whirled round when a second-child scuttled along the corridor outside. Finally he cringed before Immanence.

"Let us watch this," said Immanence, and swung back round to face the screens.

Gnores moved warily around the captain to stand at his side.

"It is unfortunate that thrall implantation in humans does not seem to be working," Immanence noted.

"But... I am obtaining some results... Father," Gnores replied.

"Results, yes, but no positive ones."

The doors into the hold opened, and a hundred second-children clattered in, led by Scrabbler who, now a fully grown first-child, loomed over his fellows. Many humans stood, but many more remained prostrate on the floor. The children did not hesitate; eager for the kill they swarmed towards the humans. Scrabbler reached them first, beheaded a man with one claw and impaled a woman on the tang of the other, then hurled her behind him. Screaming arose and the stink of human fear wafted around the sanctum from scent projectors. The man with the bone managed to stove in the head of a second child before others swarmed over him, tearing him apart. The second-children then lost themselves in frenzied abandon. Limbs, torsos and heads were flying all over the place. Immanence supposed Scrabbler would be conducting no autopsies on these humans.

Immanence eyed Gnores and saw him lifting his feet up and down and reflexively opening and closing his claws.

"Once we depart U-space, Gnores, you will take one hundred second-children in the shuttle over to the Boh runcible and secure it for me."

Gnores froze, then slowly turned his eye-palps towards his father, his mandibles vibrating. First the excitement of all the killing in the hold, and now this? Immanence understood Gnores' confusion. The captain considered killing Gnores and promoting Scrabbler, but that would be premature. It was always best to have first-child replacements ready behind each newly promoted Prime, and the captain needed to find a possible replacement for Scrabbler, though there were one or two likely second-child candidates in that hold. Equally, if he killed Gnores and sent Scrabbler to secure the runcible, and some problem arose resulting in Scrabbler being killed, he would end up with no Prime at all—a lamentable circumstance.

"You will of course kill any humans you find there. I don't think we'll be taking any more prisoners for experimentation until all the data you and Vagule collected has been analysed."

"And the human world—will I be leading assaults there?" Gnores asked, his enthusiasm returning.

"Trajeen serves no tactical purpose so, unfortunately not. We will make a close pass around the world and see how well Scrabbler's viral strains do. I won't even bomb the place, since we'll want the runcibles to continue functioning, hopefully spreading the virus throughout the Polity."

Gnores bowed down, disappointed.

"There will be other worlds, and other humans," Immanence assured him.

The door to this particular administrator's office stood open and the signs of a hasty departure were evident everywhere: memcrystals scattered on the floor from an open box, a cup of coffee spilt across a table, and a half-finished sandwich abandoned on the desk. The console on the desk linked into the complex's discrete network, but also possessed a secure connection to the Trajeen network. Most consoles here were like this. Moria did not need anything special to try what she intended, all she needed were command protocols and codes which should be available to her now. She walked over to the swivel chair and seated herself.

The records Jebel Krong made available to her were enlightening. From them she learnt about Conlan's subversion techniques. But the main thing had been simply learning that the man used an optic link directly into any system, thus making his aug more than just a discrete node in any network, but actually plugging into it and becoming more of an integral component. Mentally she sent the instruction—wordless code—to open the casing on her aug. It clicked behind her ear and she reached up to hinge open the little lid. Using a vanity mirror brought for the purpose, she found the socket and inserted one plug of an optic cable, then inserted its other plug into the requisite socket in the console.

LOGON CODE>

Could it be as simple as that?

Via her aug, Moria input her code and discovered that no, it would not be that simple.

NAME>

MORIA SALEM

MOTHER'S NAME>

GILLIAN AN-PARS SALEM

So, it seemed a lengthy question-and-answer security check would ensue—based on her record—probably followed by obscure questions concerning her personal history. However, the next question to come up was unexpected.

SOLVE> 0.004532 DISPARITY BETWEEN G3 AND G2

Now her aug flicked into full-blown modelling mode and it seemed she was again at Boh, as a virtual model of the two gates filled her perception—distances truncated as before. She created the underlying maps for gravity, system energy and U-space coordinates and placed over them models of the two runcibles' energy systems she recalled from her aug's memspace. Warp initiation. The cusps formed, the meniscus expanding as the gateposts irised apart. No cargo ship this time. She checked her figures and discovered the disparity this time to be one decimal place different from before 0.004532 rather than 0.0004532. She began to make the correction and as channels opened to her she felt elation, rather than the terror of her first experience of this. She easily opened extra processing space as the massive data flow threatened to overwhelm her. Her calculations to superpose her corrected model on reality ran easily at first, but then she realised that the decimal point made things substantially more difficult. She applied for more processing space, received it from somewhere. Almost in horror she realised that one corrective model would not be enough. She needed five. More space. Five copies made and calculations running to alter them to a stepped correction. She was getting there.

I NOW GIVE YOU TOTAL CONTROL OF THE BOH OUTER GATE >

SOLVE >

Fucking comedian!

The cargo vessel now suddenly appeared in all her models, throwing everything into disarray. Solved: model one, two, three... four and five. Through, the cargo vessel was through. Buffer feedback figures.

There!

Suddenly she realised what had gone wrong during the

real test. The energy at the meniscus, just a few points out because she did not include in the calculation the cargo vessel's transition time through the warp. It seemed so obvious, and so easy to move, in the mathematical realm, beyond it. Again she glimpsed beyond the warp seemingly into U-space itself. Terror lay there, and epiphany. Logic began to break down and it felt to her as if something tore in her head. Briefly she saw the cargo ship leaving the Boh gate, and remaining intact. Then the models began to erase one after the other.

FULL SYSTEM ACCESS

WELCOME MORIA >

Moria smiled and felt a godlike omniscience, then messages began to come through one after another:

A ROLLING STONE GATHERS NO MOSS

THROW DIRT ENOUGH, AND SOME WILL STICK

THE ROAD TO HELL IS PAVED WITH GOOD INTENTIONS

She pulled the optic lead from her aug and leapt out of the chair as if a snake had appeared on the desk.

The AI is still in the system?

No, but maybe some fragments of it remained...like George. She shouldn't let it spook her like that. Getting her breathing under control she sat down again and reconnected. The proverbs kept coming, so she routed them into memstorage in her aug and concentrated on her access to the systems controlling both runcibles. Soon she ascertained that Jebel Krong had turned off the positioning drives so that the whole complex no longer accelerated towards Trajeen. A sensible decision really, what with him intending to detonate CTD mines aboard. She tracked through the sensors previously used by the AIs and finally located two spacesuited figures working at one of the gateposts, placing a nondescript cylinder inside one of the access hatches. Moving on she began testing her control, applying models in her aug but not actually initiating any action. She could turn the positioning drives back on, here and at Boh, and she could initiate the warp, though doing that would require processing space from the Trajeen networks which were currently crammed with traffic. She possessed complete exterior control of the runcibles, though without an AI, no chance of sending anything through, so what was the point? A moment of power before the shit-storm hit, and with that power she could do nothing.

AND HAND IN HAND, ON THE EDGE OF THE SAND,

THEY DANCED BY THE LIGHT OF THE MOON,

What?

She was routing all that into storage, so why had her aug brought that one to her attention? A quick search rendered the answer to her: this was no proverb, but part of the nonsense verse penned by Edward Lear, the one Iversus Skaidon, the inventor of runcible technology, had so loved.

Why, why that?

THE MOON

THE MOON

THEY DANCED BY THE LIGHT OF THE MOON.

Hand in hand.

A shiver ran through her as she clearly visualized Jebel Krong standing haloed by Trajeen, Vina speeding over above him.

The moon.

Was she just imagining things? Groping desperately? This must be madness. But … Jebel intended to install an aug on George … would there be enough of the AI left? And those proverbs, didn't they make a weird distorted kind of sense?

Moria sat back, seemingly paralysed by the enormity of what she was thinking. Then, after a long pause, she sent the instruction to start up the positioning drives again, to speed the runcible back on its way towards Trajeen.

"Thank you, thank you so much," Jebel said, his words directed out into space to a Polity dreadnought captain called Tomalon. The news had only just reached him and at first he found it difficult to credit, but the cheering from his Avalonians seemed to drive it home. The *Occam Razor*—there a name to go down in history. A Polity ship had actually destroyed one of those fuckers. But Jebel's good mood rapidly faded. Apparently the *Occam Razor*, though still in pursuit, was severely damaged. And with Jebel's Prador ship still on the way, that victory brought no respite at all. Then other recently received information surfaced in his mind.

I guess, Cirrella, you were lucky.

The news only recently reached Jebel an hour before that about the *Occam Razor*, though it had been known after the questioning of the survivors from *Avalon Station*. The AI's best estimate of those taken aboard the Prador ship stood at around seven hundred, and Jebel wished he possessed less imagination, less of a clear vision of what might be happening to them, still happening to them. He supposed their number would be much depleted now, if any remained alive at all. Rescue was of course impossible, but now there seemed some small possibility of an ending.

Jebel up-close-and-personal Krong.

He had killed so many of them that way, sticking mines on their carapaces and blowing the bastards to bouillabaisse. In the beginning, every death brought some satisfaction, but as the war progressed and he came to realise that Prador adults cared very little about the deaths of their numerous children, his feelings of satisfaction diminished. And always *the* ship remained, with Immanence still comfortably ensconced aboard it.

This time, by mining the Boh runcible, maybe Jebel could get to the Prador captain, *really* plant an explosive on a carapace where it would hurt, for Immanence would certainly try to seize that runcible first. Or was he kidding himself? Wouldn't the Prador captain expect something like this, wouldn't he send his children to scour the Boh runcible first? Jebel frowned. Damn he wanted to go out there, just to get close to the ship, just to have the opportunity, no matter how small to—

"What is it, Urbanus?" He turned as the Golem entered the lounge.

"We are under power—the positioning drives have been restarted."

"What?" Jebel felt a flash of irritation. "Well turn them off again and cut the power supply."

"We can't. It seems they were reinstated by executive order."

It took Jebel a moment to absorb that. "Moria Salem?"

"She is the only one who could do that, unless the override came from one of the planetary AIs. One of them is presently trying to extract information from George, and it tells me no such override has been initiated."

"Bring her here—she's got some explaining to do."

"There's no need for that." Moria strode into the room.

Jebel assessed her. He had rather liked her forthright attitude and hardheaded approach to the situation they faced. He rather liked her. But now he could see she was frightened and rather less sure of herself.

She turned to Urbanus. "Have you fitted George with an aug?"

Urbanus glanced towards Jebel, who inclined his head slightly.

"I have. George is currently linked to one of the

planetary AIs."

"Have you discovered anything?" She nervously rubbed her hands together and could not conceal her disappointment when the Golem shook his head. Now she turned towards Jebel. "I think I understand it all now, but it's a matter of positioning and … this Conlan."

"Woman, you had better start making sense sometime soon or you will be joining him in his cell."

"I'm presuming Conlan possessed some means of communicating with the Prador ship when it arrives?"

"He was to use his aug to make com connection on the back of the U-space link to Boh—the runcible control signal. He's generously given me the code he intended to use, and when the Prador ship does arrive he will be informing them that he has complete control of the two runcibles. I'm hoping this will make them less diligent in searching for any nasty surprises on the Boh runcible."

"Good, that's exactly what I want."

"I won't warn you again." Jebel tried to keep it under control, but felt himself close to losing his temper. Moria seemed oblivious to this—off somewhere in her own mind.

"Positioning. You told me an ECS dreadnought is pursuing the Prador ship?"

Jebel stared down at the floor, took a deep breath and tried to find some calm within himself. "It is," he said tightly, "though it is severely damaged and I doubt it will be up to much."

"And how soon after the Prador ship will it arrive?"

"Almost on top of it, I'm told."

"It is damaged … but it should possess sufficient armament to destroy the Boh runcible?"

"Yes, but we'll be mining that, so there will be no need."

"And I should be able to communicate with that ship

from here?"

"Yes…if I give you the required frequency and codes, which I have no intention of doing until you start making sense. I've no intention—"

Jebel gaped at the apparition that now appeared in the doorway: George, with a smear of blood behind his newly installed aug, which stood open, the optic connection dangling.

Moria turned. "You know, don't you? You realised," she said.

George replied emphatically, "When one door shuts, another door opens." Then added, "Faith will move mountains."

Moria whirled back to Jebel. "That confirms it for me, do you agree?"

"Agree with *what!*" Jebel bellowed.

"Oh yes," Moria said, and told him

After availing himself of the meagre facilities, which were substantially better than those in his prior accommodation, Conlan paced the small cabin, then paused when he felt that weird shifting telling him the ship was just surfacing from U-space. A short in-system jump, then. In his estimation that meant their destination could only be one place: the Boh runcible. He considered what that might mean, but could come up with no sensible answer, so he sat down and waited. Within a few minutes the door to his cabin opened and Jebel Krong entered.

"Ah, you are considerably more sweet-smelling than when last we met," said Krong.

"Besides that," said Conlan, "and the fact that I am aboard this ship and still breathing, I rather suspect you want something from me."

The expression on Jebel's face told Conlan that only what

the man wanted prevented him from beating Conlan to a pulp. And as Conlan was well aware, Jebel Krong could easily do just that.

"As you've probably guessed, we've just arrived at the Boh runcible. Urbanus and Lindy will shortly be suiting up to conceal CTD mines throughout the structure. You and I will be going down there, where you will key in with your aug to the U-space connection. When the Prador vessel arrives you will tell its captain precisely what I instruct you to tell him."

"And why should I do this?"

"Would you like me to start becoming uncivilized again?" Jebel enquired.

"What have I got to say?"

"You'll first tell the Prador captain that you and your people now occupy the Trajeen runcible and, through it, control the Boh runcible. With the proviso that some technicians aboard the Trajeen runcible have managed to evade you, though you'll state that they should not be a problem."

"Then?"

"When the time comes I'll inform you."

"Well, I won't say what you want, not without certain guarantees."

"I can offer you one guarantee." Krong pulled two objects from the pocket of the light spacesuit he now wore and tossed them down on the nearby cabin bed: a pair of pliers and a pair of metal snips.

Conlan stared at the two tools, his mouth arid. "Yes… you can hurt me, but that won't help you get what you want. If I'm in pain I won't have much aug control, but even if I do, I might forget some key phrases necessary for me to use with that Prador captain, to assure him that I am not being coerced."

"What is it you want, then?" Krong asked, teeth gritted.

Conlan decided it was time for him to find out how strong his bargaining position might be. Obviously Krong wanted him to convince the Prador that he controlled the runcibles so they would take one of them aboard without sufficiently checking it. Maybe he was integral to this desperate plan. Now he would find out. "I want a new identity, and all records of my old identity wiped. I want two million New Carth shillings paid to me in etched sapphires, and an unrecorded runcible transmission to any destination of my choosing."

"Oh, is that all?" Jebel asked. "How about a Marineris Trench apartment, a new wardrobe and couple of courtesans to feed you peeled grapes?"

"If I thought all my demands would be met I'd ask for your testicles on a metal hook," Conlan spat.

"Really," Krong leant over him, very close, as if wishing Conlan would attack. "Here's the deal, Conlan: you get to live. You get adjustment and a custodial sentence reviewed every ten years."

"No way is any AI going to fuck with my mind. No deal."

"Then there's only one other option." Krong stepped away from him, stooped and picked up the two tools from the bed.

Conlan wondered if he had pushed just a little too hard. Maybe adjustment wouldn't be so bad…

Krong continued, waving the metal snips at him. "This ship carries cold-sleep escape pods. You do what I say and one of them is yours. We fire it into deep space and maybe, sometime in the far future, someone will find that pod and open it. You could be lucky. The Polity could be gone by then. Or if it still exists you and your crimes might have been forgotten."

Conlan eyed those snips. That wasn't so bad. If Krong had acceded to his initial demands Conlan would have known the man intended to renege. This sounded real.

"You have a deal," he said.

The U-space transmitter did not look particularly impressive, just a grey box sitting on the floor with numerous optics and s-con power cables feeding into it. But the technology that box contained was akin to a miniature replica of the one driving the huge runcible outside the chainglass windows on this side of the complex. The transmission of information being a considerably less complex procedure than transmitting huge cargo vessels, the transmitter required no AI—a simple synaptic computer served the same purpose.

Moria chose this particular room in which to base herself, since there was less of a chance of a breakdown of the single link between this console and transmitter in here. Any other console in the complex would have been routed through other networked com nodes, and she really didn't need some idiot software glitch getting in the way. She had more than enough to do.

"Sit there." Moria pointed to one of the three chairs behind the console desk, and George meekly walked over and ensconced himself. "And no more proverbs for the moment. I know what to do now and I don't want you confusing the issue."

George seemed about to say something, but instead clamped his mouth closed like a naughty child and removed his optic cable from his top pocket. While she watched he plugged one end into his aug, then the other end into the console, then sat with his hands in his lap. He appeared childish only for a moment longer, then straightened, something metallic gleaming in his eyes.

Moria placed her flask of coffee and cup down on the pseudo-wood surface and took the chair next to him. In her aug she again checked the time. Jebel had reached the Boh runcible some hours ago, and should soon be docking to what remained of the complex there. The Prador ship would arrive in approximately five hours, according to reports from the ground-based AIs—their data obtained from monitoring stations launched throughout the Polity some days into the war. She had received no communication from the *Occam Razor*, but then U-com became difficult from within U-space—a problem the AIs hoped to iron out sometime soon.

Moria plugged herself in and began running diagnostic checks on the huge and intricate systems she controlled. She ran up every fusion reactor in the complex to its maximum, routing power into storage in the runcible buffers at this end. Solar collector satellites stood ready to maser energy to the receivers on the runcible, should she require it—a highly likely possibility. Beginning to model the two runcible gates and all the energy systems involved, she slotted in the information revealed by the diagnostic returns. Then, because she knew she was procrastinating, she took a long, hard look at her data map. Certainly the planetary AIs would release processing space to her, but it was not that area of processing that most concerned her. She closely studied the nexus of the data map, where the AI should be, and where before lay nothing but errors and broken connections. Something now occupied the space, directly linked to the console before which she sat. It looked skeletal, with at present un-instated connection to that processing space on the planet below. It looked nothing like an AI, nothing like anything she had ever seen before. It was George.

"Are you ready?" she asked—through her aug.

"Set a beggar on horseback, and he'll ride to the Devil."

There, another proverb. What other reply to expect? Whatever the hell that meant she supposed it to be the best answer she would receive.

Moria set to work calculating orbital velocities and trajectories. At present the runcible face lay at a tangent to Trajeen, so she needed to turn it to ninety degrees from the surface. Sending the cargo ship through required a two-kilometre extension of the gate; now she needed an excess of two hundred kilometres. She worked out that this would take, with each gatepost travelling at its maximum of twelve hundred kph, averaged over the distance, more than five minutes.

Too long.

A particular fact niggling at her for some time now came to the forefront of her mind. Her plan stood a much better chance of working if she could initiate the warp only after the gateposts reached full extension. This meant her accuracy in positioning the posts needed to be well inside the tolerances set for the normal method of opening the gate. Over the next long hour she calculated what the new tolerances should be, and applied them to the system. Immediately thousands of errors appeared—possibly more than she could deal with.

"*Two wrongs don't make a right,*" George told her, then added a proverb he used before, "*When one door shuts, another door opens.*"

Moria sat for long minutes trying to understand that, then abruptly felt very stupid. She did not need to initiate warp at full extension at *both* gates, only the Boh one. This cut the errors by half and, she felt, brought the required calculations within parameters she could handle. She spent a further hour modelling gate operation under these circumstances, then saved the model. Now, to position this gate.

Where it ultimately ended up around Trajeen depended

on when the Prador ship arrived and when it could be manoeuvred into position. However, she could run a rough projection based on an arrival time five hours hence. This she did, and then she began to move.

The positional drives fired up again and, slowly, through the nearby windows, she observed Trajeen rise, its blue curve filling the lower half of the view. The moment the runcible lay upright to the surface, and stabilized, she fired the drives in a different direction to send it in orbit around the planet, so it would arrive in position in five hours. Further adjustments would then be required, utterly dependent on the situation out at Boh. Now, with one of her models being updated in real-time via the U-space link and the test viewing sensors out at Boh, she observed Jebel Krong's ship docking, and waited.

Consciousness returned by slow degrees, and during moments in the in-between state, Tomalon possessed no conception of being human. He *was* the *Occam Razor*. Through its sensors he observed the Trajeen system as a whole, not contracted to human perception, and realised what mere specks were himself, and the Prador ship millions of kilometres ahead. Then the lines of division impinged, for he did not control his own body, and he became aware of Occam.

"U-space currents have affected the duration of our journey. We have arrived two hours earlier than expected," Occam told him.

"Is this a problem?"

"It is, but one that can hopefully be resolved. I am presently in communication with Moria Salem, who controls the cargo runcibles. She has transmitted a plan of which you need to be aware."

The information arrived at Tomalon's interface with

the ship AI, and he slowly and carefully worked his way through it. He felt a shiver when he began to realise what this woman intended to do, and what would be required of the *Occam Razor*.

"This is a serious proposition?" he asked.

"It is."

"So we must continuously feed her information concerning our position and the position of the Prador ship, while we make an attack run on the Boh runcible?"

As he asked this, Tomalon began checking through the ship's systems and infrastructure to see what Occam had done while he was unconscious. Various ship's robots were busily working, strengthening or replacing structural members, taking wrecked machinery and burnt and twisted metal to interior autofactories to be cut up, smelted, and turned into replacement components for the ship. A veritable swarm of constructors presently worked its way around the hull, removing damaged plates and welding new ones into place. Others were replacing looms of fried optics and wiring. A whole weapons turret had been rebuilt. Yet he realised the ship would probably not survive a head-on encounter with the Prador vessel.

"I am beginning that run now. We will swing around the Prador ship to begin it. Ascertaining our intent, Immanence will accelerate and arrive there before us."

"Well that's just dandy," Tomalon replied, wondering if he should transmit updates to his will and what the chances were of his body being found.

Urbanus and Lindy suited up and departed through the ship's outer airlock into vacuum, each carrying four CTDs. Jebel observed them for a little while on the cockpit subscreen fed from an exterior camera. Their air jets flipped out little dissolving trails as they split up, each heading for different areas of the runcible to conceal their lethal parcels. He considered waiting another hour before going to get Conlan and taking him inside the Boh complex. Then Moria made contact:

"Jebel, the Prador ship just arrived early. Already they are transmitting on the frequency Conlan gave you. You must get him to reply ASAP. Prador vessel's ETA at Boh is probably less than an hour once it gets underway—it is holding off at present."

"*That's two hours early.*" Jebel leapt up from his seat and, collecting his weapons, headed back through the ship.

"Yeah, I spotted that."

"Can you still do it?"

"I can, I think, but if I can't you still have your chance with the mines."

"Though I very much wanted to be here, the plan was that we positioned the mines then ran. One hour doesn't give us much time to do that."

"That last fact would not have been changed had you decided to ignore me."

"Yeah, I guess."

"I will be out of com henceforth. I'm going to be juggling with quite enough balls as it is. Best of luck, Jebel Krong."

"*Juggling balls—nice analogy,*" he replied, but the connection closed before he could say any more, and now he stood at the door to Conlan's room. Before entering Jebel initiated his comlink:

"Okay you two, get those mines positioned in double quick time—we've got company."

"It's here?" Lindy asked.

"Two hours early," Urbanus added.

"My words exactly," Jebel replied. "Now, you've no time to run checks. Get them positioned and get back here fast. I want you both back aboard within half an hour."

Now, through his aug, Jebel checked the view through the concealed cameras in Conlan's room, just as he had before entering the man's cell back in the Trajeen complex. Supine on the bed the man did not seem preparing some ambush this time. Jebel opened the door and entered.

"Okay, time to go."

Conlan sat upright, and Jebel studied him with what he knew to be ill-concealed contempt. Thus far he had learnt that Conlan was a hit man for some gangster organization on Trajeen before joining the Separatists. He was brave, that being a job requirement, but did not possess the kind of face-to-face bravery Jebel saw at the front. A knife in the back or the lengthy torture of a bound victim being more his style. Jebel wondered how he would fare with a laser carbine and a few gecko mines up against a Prador.

"By your hasty demeanour I suspect they have arrived?"

"You suspect right." Jebel stepped aside and drawing his thin-gun waved Conlan to the door. The killer shrugged, stood and walked over, eyeing the weapon as he passed. Jebel supposed he had considered going for it and rejected the idea. "The airlock is down there on the left."

"Do I get a suit like yours?" Conlan asked as they entered the corridor.

"No need. This lock leads directly into the Boh complex."

Reaching the lock, Jebel gestured for Conlan to open it. The exterior door already stood open, having been shunted aside for the embarkation tunnel to connect. They pulled themselves through the tunnel in zero gee, then finally clumped down on the grav-plates in a short tunnel leading to a junction with one of the complex's corridors.

"Go right."

The corridor led past accommodation units for the runcible staff, and finally terminated in a secondary Control

Centre, previously in operation while the runcible was being built, but closed down when the AI took control. Moria had, however, since brought this place back online.

"Choose a console."

Conlan moved ahead, shrugged, then plumped himself down beside the nearest console. Jebel removed an optic cable from one of his pockets and tossed it to the man.

"Remember—your life depends on what you do next."

"Oh I do understand that."

While Conlan opened up his aug and plugged in, Jebel studied his surroundings. A row of screens to his right gave him a clear view across the runcible, with Boh, the gas giant, looming behind. Within the room a horseshoe of consoles faced a bank of screens, many of which were running tech data way above Jebel's knowledge; some however, showed different views outside. On one he could see a spacesuited figure busily at work undoing an access hatch, elasticised lines holding the figure in place. By the size and shape he guessed that to be Lindy. Another screen showed a partial view of their docked ship and still others showed star-speckled blackness. He returned his attention to Conlan.

The man now sat bolt upright, his eyes closed. Speaking out loud he delivered the message as instructed, though if anything lay hidden in his words, Jebel guessed he wouldn't know until too late.

"Yes, I have control of the Trajeen cargo runcible, and through it, control of the Boh cargo runcible.... There are a few technicians still aboard here at Trajeen, but— No, they can't—not with the AI knocked out.... No, none on the Boh runcible. You are clear to take it.... Yes, I look forwards to that."

The conversation was brief, and of course much more than Conlan's life depended on it. The lives of nearly a billion souls hung in the balance. Conlan leant back and opened his eyes. "Y'know, even from a translation you can pick up a lot.

"Oh yes."

Conlan turned to face him. "Unless your mines work, everyone is going to die here. I reckon I stand the better chance in a cold coffin in vacuum."

Maybe the man believed that. Probably they were weasel words to try and get Jebel to drop his guard a little.

"So what else do I have to tell him?"

"In a little while you'll tell Immanence that those few technicians remaining aboard the Trajeen cargo runcible have managed to seize back some control, specifically of the positional drives of the Boh runcible." Jebel turned to look at him. "Those technicians will fire up those drives to open the Boh gate."

"I don't understand."

"You don't have to," Jebel told him.

8.

And hand in hand, on the edge of the sand–

Great, now she was getting a headache, which added to the feeling, despite her having applied for and received planetary processing space, of her head being filled to bursting point. Despite the early arrival of the Prador vessel, it had been necessary to slow the runcible's orbital speed to bring it to the right place at the right time. All her previous calculations she'd completely erased, since they no longer applied, even very roughly. The calculations she presently ran were a living thing. She knew the result, the solution, but necessarily needed to keep altering the input values in keeping with data received from the *Occam Razor* and the test sensors out at Boh. Sometimes, deep in all this, she lost sight of her ultimate aims, but looking out through her own eyes at the changing horizon, storms and cloud banks passing underneath her, snapped her back to reality. If she failed, that view might well change, horribly.

Returning her attention to the Trajeen runcible she again checked her preparations, hesitated for only a moment, then initiated the Skaidon warp. Her view altered immediately as the shimmering meniscus flickered into being beside her. Though the present drain on the fusion reactors lay within acceptable limits, she knew that later the need would rise beyond those limits, so onlined extra power from the solar collector satellites. The power they supplied, by maser, to the gateposts, slotted into her calculations and gave her greater manoeuvring space. She now gave the instruction for the gateposts to begin parting, though she did not yet intend to throw them out to their full extent, since their tendency to drift while the entire runcible was being moved could wreck everything. She now considered some other calculations.

The C energy, though not a true representation of what would instantiate beyond the meniscus because of the exponential progression that took place actually at the meniscus, was very substantial. Moria briefly considered taking the Boh runcible buffers completely offline, ran some calculations, and felt a sudden thrill of horror at the results this rendered. The Boh gate itself would last about .005 of a second, and it seemed possible the entire energy burst could actually ignite the gas giant itself—turn it into a small, swiftly burning sun. Not a great idea. She could not do that; however, she did not have to work the gate as intended for the transmission of cargo ships. The output velocity did not have to be the same as the input, for she could borrow some of the C energy and add it to the latter.

The energy calculation ran roughly at a 70,000 kph disparity between the Trajeen and Boh gates, so anything entering the Trajeen gate at, say, 10 kph, would exit Boh at 70,010 kph, so an object travelling at 40,000 would exit at 110,000… Moria calculated the extent of possible damage to the Boh runcible, and to various objects within its vicinity. She based these calculations on probable reaction times of Prador systems and the Prador themselves. She factored in the probable breakup of a certain object when accelerated beyond certain limits, including in those factors the results of geological surveys requested from the planetary network, and in the end settled on borrowing one fortieth of the C energy. Very roughly, C equalled 1,070,000,000 kph. One fortieth plus initial velocities resulted in a total of twenty-seven million kilometres per hour. In one second, an object travelling at that speed, would cover 7500 kilometres. As Moria modelled the near future, the scene, playing out in her mind, lit a fire behind her eyes.

While some second-children brought him lunch, Immanence ruefully observed the Polity dreadnought, and damned himself for not turning back to destroy it when it was more badly damaged than this. He had mistakenly believed it to be either a lifeless hulk or crippled beyond the ability to go anywhere, and transmitted its location to other, smaller, Prador vessels, thinking it now a problem beneath his notice. However, its presence here did not particularly worry him, because even scanning from a distance it appeared the damage was by no means completely repaired. It might be able to travel, but if it actually tried to attack he knew he could destroy it.

He continued studying the vessel while he mulled over the recent message from the human Separatist. As per plan they had seized control of the Trajeen cargo runcible, and because of that the Boh runcible was now his for the taking. He decided that when he finally travelled inwards to Trajeen itself, he would send Gnores or Scrabbler to collect those Separatists, to bring them aboard for dinner... But that pleasant prospect lay in the future, meanwhile he must decide what to do about this damned Polity ship. Should he turn back and destroy it before seizing the Boh runcible, or just continue with his mission here and destroy it should it try to engage? The latter, he decided.

As Immanence directed his chouds to set his own vessel on a course for Boh, he still kept sensors directed towards the enemy ship and realised, from its trajectory, that it was not, as expected, trying to intercept him. It swung out and round, accelerating hard. The Prador captain felt a sudden amusement. Obviously the Polity ship's captain intended to give himself as much time as possible to make further repairs, and then await Immanence as part of some organized defence of Trajeen itself. Typical of the desperate measures these humans took to protect their own. Immanence munched contemplatively on the human leg a second-child passed up to his mandibles. Then, another possibility occurred to him.

His stomachs rumbled, and he released a long acidic belch, simultaneously spitting the leg out, down onto the second-child's carapace. With a sweep of his claw he sent the child squalling and tumbling end over end into the wall. Too much of a good thing in two respects: the rich human meat was beginning to have an unwanted effect on his digestion, and easy victories led him into a stupid complacency. He realised the Polity captain must know the runcibles were now controlled by Separatists and divined Immanence's plan concerning the one at Boh, and was racing ahead to take control of or even destroy that runcible before Immanence could seize it.

The Prador captain sent the instruction for maximum acceleration, and even in his grav-plated and shock-absorbing sanctum felt the surge throughout the ship as two extra fusion engines fired up and flamed out into space. Champing his mandibles he checked the navigational projections, and slowly his irritation receded. The Polity ship was fast, but not quite fast enough. Immanence would arrive before it. He now opened com channels:

"Gnores, get aboard the shuttle and prepare for launch when we arrive."

"Yes, Father."

Immanence now returned his attention to the quivering second-children attending him. "Bring me shorefish and boulder eel steaks. I've had enough of this human meat for now."

The second-children scurried away.

Jebel observed Lindy and Urbanus returning to the ship well within the time he allotted them, but a glance at the screens in this Control Centre only confirmed the message just received from the dreadnought captain: the Prador ship was accelerating massively, and now the Boh runcible lay well within its sensor range. Plans needed to change.

Jebel accessed the blueprint of this runcible complex in his aug and searched for a likely place of concealment. Much of the structure was missing and the complex here was nowhere near as large as the one at Trajeen. He checked corridor plans, the layouts of various accommodation units, then finally settled on a secluded garden, not because it was the best place to hide, but because it lay under a chainglass dome and would present them with a grand view of near-future events. Of course, an airlock lay nearby as well.

"Urbanus, Lindy, when you get back inside, grab armament and all the chameleonware you can find, and head for this location." Via his aug he sent the relevant map references. "You should be able to get there quicker by going outside again. Oh, and bring another spacesuit."

"The reason for this?" Urbanus enquired.

"The Prador ship accelerated and now we are well within the range of its sensors. We can't leave."

Silence met this, and Jebel knew what the other two were thinking. If they left the runcible now, this would result in their probable destruction by weapons fired from the Prador ship. Their presence here would make Immanence infinitely suspicious, so he would ensure that no booby traps lay aboard the runcible. But most importantly he would also regard Conlan's information as suspect, because Conlan had told the Prador this runcible was secure. The ship docked outside did not matter, since it could have been abandoned during the evacuation, but their presence did. Jebel realised they were now utterly committed to Moria's plan, and must conceal themselves from the Prador to see it through.

"I am not sure that I relish the prospect of staying here," Conlan opined.

"Live with it," Jebel spat.

Conlan stood. "If we don't run now we'll be found, and if we are not found we'll end up inside that ship with all your mines. That wasn't part of the deal. I didn't sign on for a suicide mission."

Jebel considered violence, and rejected it. He still needed Conlan to speak to the Prador captain again. It might be a critical key, considering the level of Prador paranoia. He turned to the man, nodded to the door and with his thin-gun waved Conlan ahead of him.

"I don't for one moment think that Immanence, given time to check things and properly secure his position, will allow those mines inside his ship. So we are going to panic him. Right now there's a Polity dreadnought heading here. You will send a message to Immanence telling him that those controlling the positional drives intend to open up the Boh runcible, wide, to present a larger target for the Polity dreadnought's weapons." Jebel halted, spotting something on one of the screens. The Prador ship was now visible, as was the shuttle now departing it.

Conlan turned, glanced towards the same screen then focused his attention back on Jebel. "I'm not sure I see the point of such a message."

Jebel waved him on towards the door. "Immanence will try to protect all or part of the runcible. This means he'll get close, perhaps close enough to be damaged by those mines. He may even risk grabbing all or part of the runcible. In which case we have him."

Jebel considered the explanation he had just given. Not bad on the spur of the moment. He did not want to risk telling Conlan the whole truth until the last moment—didn't want to give the man too much time to think about it and see all its holes, then maybe slip something else into his message to the Prador.

"But where will we be when this happens?"

Jebel mulled his answer over for a moment, then decided to go right to it. "I promised you a chance to survive this, and I will stick to my word. As you heard: the others will be bringing a spare spacesuit for you."

"And?" Conlan asked.

"Though my dislike of the Prador drives me to do things some would consider suicidal, I do actually want to continue living," said Jebel. "You'll make contact with Immanence, tell him what I just told you, and once that's done there's no more reason for us to remain here. If we tried leaving by ship, that would alert the Prador. So we don't leave by ship."

"What?"

Jebel continued: "There's one horror for anyone who ever goes EVA in a spacesuit. It's the idea of your line breaking or you being flung away into vacuum. What happens then? You float through space and gradually run out of air, dying a pretty horrible death."

"But that doesn't happen," said Conlan.

"Precisely," Jebel replied. "When in that situation you can now initiate the suit's injector pack. The drugs throw you into a hibernation state in which you use less than five per cent of the suit's oxygen. Out here your power supply would run out before the oxygen, and in that hibernation state you would freeze. People have actually been revived from that."

"You're insane," said Conlan, coming to a halt.

Jebel shook his head. "If we stay here, we die either when the mines detonate or the Prador find us. Leaving through an airlock we just might slip under the radar—too small to notice. At least this way we'll have some chance, not much different from the chance I offered you before, Conlan."

"Freezing in a suit is not quite the same as being put in suspended animation in a cold coffin."

Jebel shrugged. "Tough," he said, and prodded Conlan in the back with his gun barrel to get him moving again.

As he walked, Conlan realised Jebel Krong had not revealed all his plans, but he just could not fathom the rest. It sounded good—initiating an action to drive Immanence into grabbing the mined runcible without thoroughly checking it—but stood no chance of success. The Prador were winning. Why would Immanence risk his entire ship just for the dubious gain of this technology? It all seemed just too desperate. The Prador hammer was coming down and he, Krong and Trajeen itself were sitting on the anvil. Time for him to alter things in his favour.

A shuttle now approached from the Prador ship. Having loaded the plans of this complex while linked in with his aug, Conlan guessed that shuttle would dock at the largest access point—a small embarkation lounge about three-quarters of a kilometre from where he stood. He modelled his own position on those plans and considered imminent actions. His chances of escaping once he and Krong joined the other two would drop to zero, not simply because there would be three of them, but because one of them was a Golem and could move very fast when required.

Linking into this complex's systems was easy, and he had done it in parallel while he spoke to Immanence. Of course he possessed no executive control, for that operated from Trajeen and whoever held the reins there. But he did not need to control the runcible itself—nothing large like that—all he needed was the level of system control available to a maintenance technician. Ahead, lay a crossroads. The right-hand corridor led to a storeroom, the left-hand one terminated at a drop-shaft leading either up or down to further levels. In his aug Conlan set up three instructions: one a simple radio transmission to a junction box a little way ahead of him, the other to set in motion a light-intensifier program to run the moment he sent the first signal, and the third to signal another critical junction box in the left-hand corridor. Conlan sent the first signal and put out the lights.

The shots cut the air overhead as Conlan dropped and flung himself forwards. He rolled into the left-hand corridor as further shots slammed into the wall next to him, their impact sites leaving black shadows in his aug-intensified vision. Within a few strides he reached the drop-shaft and hit the panel to initiate the irised gravity field to take him upwards, and dove into the shaft. Jebel pursued closely, and one pulse from his thin-gun took off Conlan's boot heel as he rose out of sight. Now Conlan abruptly reached out and grabbed a maintenance ladder beside the shaft. Jebel, into the shaft below, spinning round to aim up at him. Third signal. The drop-shaft's power cut out, and the grav-plates on lower levels exerted their pull. Jebel yelled and dropped. There followed a sickening crack Conlan easily recognised as the sound of bone breaking, and another yell. Conlan began climbing just as fast as he could. Thin-gun shots threw sparks up the shaft as he exited on the next floor. Conlan ran.

Immanence watched as the shuttle, containing Gnores and the second-children, decelerated towards the Boh runcible. Under a similar decelerating burn his own vessel shook and grumbled all around him. However it carried a great deal more inertia than the shuttle and relative to its mass its engines were smaller, so it needed to lose velocity around Boh before coming back into position between the runcible and the approaching Polity ship. Immanence champed in frustration, once again belched acid, and damned all humans. While the deceleration continued he summoned Scrabbler and one other to him.

"Are you ready to take on the position as Prime?" he asked the first-child.

Scrabbler danced about a little. "Yes, Father. Yes I am."

"The Polity ship may fire on the Boh runcible. In the unlikelihood that I do not intercept all its missiles, it is quite possible that Gnores will not survive. You will then be Prime. I'll want you to ready the second shuttle for a similar mission to the Trajeen runcible. One has to prepare…"

"Now, should I do it now…Father?" Scrabbler could hardly contain his glee.

The second individual Immanence summoned now reached the doors into the sanctum and waited there indecisively. Immanence waved that one in with his claw. Scrabbler turned and eyed this second-child—one grown slightly larger than usual.

"XF-458, come before me. Scrabbler, you may depart."

Scrabbler turned and headed for the doors with uncertain steps, his eye-palps quivering, and perhaps now he had some intimation of the extent of his father's preparations.

Staring down at the thriving second-child before him, Immanence pondered how many times he had done this before. Scrabbler would be his forty-third Prime … or was that fifty-third?

"XF-458, you will henceforth be known as Gurnax," Immanence began. Later, when he dismissed the new first-child, who was not quite grown enough to assume that title, he checked other likely candidates amongst the remaining second-children and sent instructions redirecting them to different food stores within the ship. He then ordered some third-children to be thawed out and placed in the nursery. Preparation was everything.

By the time the runcible rose back into sight around Boh, the shuttle had finally docked. Immanence chose a course to bring him between Boh and the runcible, then to a stable orbit between the runcible and the approaching Polity dreadnought. With an inner smile he noted launches from the other vessel—a swarm of rail-gun missiles.

Should have fired those earlier, he thought.

Some tinkering with steering thrusters brought him much closer to the runcible, so the Polity ship could obtain no clear line of sight to that structure. The rail-gun missiles, hurtling in at a terrific velocity, could not change their course. A few hours later they began impacting on the exotic metal hull. Immanence noted minimal damage and a steady increase in power available to his particle cannons. Then he detected launches of self-powered missiles from the approaching vessel. These would be more of a danger because they could be programmed to swing round and come in from any direction, and could even shut down for a little while, drift, then start up their drives again for a renewed attack. Immanence drew his ship even closer to the structure and onlined masers and meteor lasers, then sent an order to another part of the ship: "You will intercept and destroy any missiles that get past this ship. I am sending you each your areas of deployment. Nothing must get past. Is that understood?"

A concert of voices replied, "Yes, Father."

Gazing through sensors in the drone cache, Immanence watched the nine spherical war drones accelerating out through the triangular space door. Checking designations he noted Vagule was the last of them. This must be just chance, for Vagule could now have no sense of trying to extend his span. Via exterior sensors the captain watched them speeding away, the proximity to the runcible being such that Boh cast a weak shadow over them and the ship. Now Immanence returned his attention to the approaching enemy.

"Bring it on human," he bubbled in the Prador tongue. "Just come a little closer."

Gnores hurtled from the assault docking tube punched through the skin of the station, and scrambled to a halt tearing up carpet in the embarkation lounge. He swung in a circle, rail-gun, particle weapon and a laser brought to bear on the branching corridors around him. He felt rather reckless and quite relished the prospect of a fight. It was a first-child trait, and another reason why first-children tended to need replacing. He knew this, but still could not feel any other way, just as he knew that his father might be preparing to remove him, and could do nothing but obey.

Fifty second-children now poured in, similarly armed but also carrying high-powered scanners. No attack revealed itself—not a human in sight.

"Follow the search pattern precisely. Those who deviate, unless required to by combat, will not be returning to Father's ship," Gnores told them. But if there was anything to find he did not expect it to be within these human accommodation units. The other fifty second-children, suited against vacuum and now spreading out around the entire structure, would be the ones to find booby traps, because if they were here, they would certainly be on the runcible device itself.

Gnores replaced all his weapons in his harness, then while walking around the embarkation lounge, listened into the com-chatter of the second-children, and to those channels open back to the ship, which kept him updated. Moving over to a wide window—something unthinkable to a Prador for here would be a weakness in its armour—he gazed at his father's ship, clearly visible just out from the runcible. The ship stood silhouetted against gaseous incandescence on its other side, and through those channels Gnores learnt it was intercepting a rail-gun attack.

"Gnores! Gnores! Gnores! A human!"

Gnores whirled around and accelerated across the lounge to the branching corridors on the other side. Many of them were far too small for him to enter. Besides, he did not know which one he should enter anyway.

On the com unit he now held in his claw, Gnores traced who spoke, reaching forward with one of his finer underhands to manipulate the complex controls. XG-12, one of the batch raised to second-childhood shortly after they set out from the Second Kingdom. According to the map he should be a hundred metres over—

The human charged into sight with XG-12 snapping claws at his heels. Gnores drew and aimed his rail-gun, but then realised the human was unarmed. The creature paused, seeing him, then abruptly ran towards him, making all sorts of strange noises and waving about its soft upper limbs.

"Desist, XG-12. Return to the search."

The second-child slid to a halt, perhaps remembering Gnores' earlier threat and realising that this might not be defined as a combat situation. It turned away and ran off. The human staggered to a halt before Gnores, gasping, and still intermittently making those noises. Gnores realised it was trying to talk to him, only he carried no translator. He reached out and closed the tips of his claws on its lower torso and picked it up.

"Father, I have found a human. It is trying to speak to me but I do not understand it," he sent via one of the channels to the ship.

After a moment Immanence, having viewed Gnores' prize through the cameras mounted on the first-child's carapace, replied, "Gnores, it is not trying to speak to you. It is making those sounds because it is in pain. You have damaged it."

Gnores abruptly realised he had squeezed too tightly, for the lower torso of the creature split open and organs were bulging out. There also seemed to be a lot of red liquid dribbling onto the floor. Gnores dropped the human at once. He observed it coiling on its side and trying to push its internal organs back inside.

"I was sure it was trying to speak to me a moment ago," he said.

"Why do you not have a translator with you?" Immanence enquired.

Gnores felt a sudden flash of embarrassment. Though having brought every variety of hand weapon, scanning gear and equipment for accessing human computer systems, he had entirely forgotten about bringing a translator. Then came the fear. Father would severely punish such a lapse. Such a lapse would probably ensure his removal as a Prime. And there was only one way Primes were *ever* removed.

"But this place was supposed to be empty! My mission here was to scan for booby traps and secure—"

"Upon your return, Gnores," said Immanence, "we will discuss this further."

Gnores sagged as the comlink broke. He stared dimly into his future and realised it did not extend very far. *Damned human!* He sank into a fug of self-pity and wondered if his father was already ordering a drone shell to be brought up to his sanctum, or if all of Gnores would be food for second-children. *The human*—some payback there... Gnores forced his attention back to his surroundings. He would keep the human alive. He would be much more careful this time.

Maybe he could make that pleasure last until Immanence recalled him. He peered down at the floor and saw a bloody trail leading over to a nearby corridor, the human just dragging himself from sight. Gnores charged over and crashed into the corridor mouth—his shell too large to allow him ingress. For a moment he tore at the walls with his claws, but then the human opened some kind of access hatch and began pulling himself inside. Gnores drew his rail-gun and fired, but too late, for the human escaped.

Gnores stood grinding his mandibles together and drooling black saliva. After a moment he pushed himself back and whirled away. No matter. It wouldn't live very long with such injuries. They never did.

Now. The time was now. Moria restarted the positioning drives on the Trajeen runcible, and observed the massive gateposts separating from each other, slowly at first then accelerating, drawing out the Skaidon warp, the drives' white blades of flame pointing inwards over the meniscus surface. In her real-time model Moria observed the *Occam Razor* hurtling down towards Boh, and the Prador vessel dropping lower and lower to keep itself between its opponent and the runcible. Some of the Polity vessel's missiles came close to hitting the runcible itself. That would spell disaster, but, equally, revealing to the Prador that the Boh runcible was not the Polity ship's intended target would be disastrous too. But just maybe there lay a way around that. Moria accessed the runcible's meteor collision lasers and routed through to them a military ballistics program uploaded from the planet. Maybe that would be enough.

Now the Boh runcible. She started the positional drives there, and watched the ring of white fire bloom. Conlan should be sending the second signal now. She did not have time to check with Jebel, and checking would not change matters.

Utterly unbelievable pain, almost equalled by the horror of being injured like that. Okay now, all wrapped up and back where it should be. The Prador had pinched his abdomen tightly in the tips of its claws, too tight. If it had gripped him only slightly differently it would have snapped his spine. His bulging guts pressed hard against the serrated inner edges of the claw, which cut in, and his intestines and the lower lobes of his liver belched through the split. He'd got it all back inside, and with the remains of his shirt bound it all in place, and tied that down with the optic cable, but the blood just kept oozing out. He was bleeding internally too. He could feel it. Death did not lie very far away.

EDDRESS REQUEST >

OFFLINE EDDRESS REQUEST?

ACCEPT?

"What the fuck?" he managed. He looked around at the cramped space, could hear the clattering sound of hard Prador feet not very far away. Perhaps they wanted to exchange messages, for they seemed quite anxious to reacquaint themselves with him. Conlan damned himself for a fool. The moment he saw one of those little bastards face-to-face he knew that running to them had been a suicidal move. The big one, like the one called Vortex appearing on the newsnets, he assumed to be a leader of some kind. Why hadn't it listened to him?

The eddress request remained and he considered taking the facility offline, but what the hell did it matter now? He accepted and immediately received a message:

YOU BROKE MY FUCKING LEG YOU PIECE OF SHIT.

VOCAL CONNECTION?

Conlan accepted that and sent, *"I hope it really hurts. You still at the bottom of that shaft?"*

"No, Urbanus came and collected me and now I've a couple of nice drug patches on my chest—compound fracture, so pretty nasty. He got the bones back into my leg and splinted it. I don't seem to mind that you've probably screwed this operation."

Conlan felt he could do with some similar patches himself. Obviously, by his tone over the link, Jebel Krong floated up in the clouds.

"I'll tell you what. I haven't screwed your operation completely, but I still can. You send Urbanus for me, with some of those patches, and maybe I'll still do what you want." As he finished delivering that speech, Conlan realised that if speaking out loud he would have needed to pause for breath every few words.

Jebel's laughter came ghostly over the link. *"So the Prador weren't talking? Have they got you now, stuck you up on a wall somewhere? You really won't like what happens next. Remember me telling you?"*

"They don't have me. I'm in hiding. I'm serious about my offer."

"No can do, I'm afraid. This place is crawling with them. We're under a chameleonware shield, local, blocking scan. No intention of moving right now. They'll probably find you soon enough. Bit of advice for you..."

"What's that?"

"Kill yourself."

"You are a bastard, Krong."

Laughter again, then, *"And you're not?"*

Conlan looked around. He lay in an air duct junction. The Prador might pick him up on their scanners, but they'd have to cut through a lot of metalwork to reach him. By then he could crawl on to somewhere else.

"How long till the runcible starts moving?" he asked.

"Any time now."

"If I send your signal, and survive ... will you hold to your promise to me?"

"Of course, but I don't really see you surviving. Are you near a console now?"

Conlan wasn't, but further along a nearby duct a vent opened into some private accommodation and there would be one in there. He considered his survival chances. It would be so much easier to lie here and die; already he felt slightly cold and sleepy. Approaching the Prador again would almost certainly result in the scenario Krong once described to him and promised to mimic with pliers and metal snips. If he crawled to that room and sent the signal, Krong's plan might succeed. But then there were the Prador here. In that room he would be more vulnerable and he doubted he would be able to haul himself up to the vent again.

"Tell me again your plan?" he asked.

"Oh, you mean about the mines and such—all complete bollocks, obviously."

"What?"

"Well, I didn't want you telling your Prador chums. The mine scenario worked just fine for our purposes. And even if you ratted on us the real plan might still work."

"So what is your real plan?"

"You expect me to tell you now? Why should I do that?"

"Because my guts are hanging out, I'm bleeding internally, and I know the Prador are not my chums."

"Love the Polity now do you?"

"I hate it and all it stands for, but right now I hate the Prador more."

After a long pause Jebel spoke more soberly. *"Give me a visual link via your aug, and patch in a med diagnostic."*

"Med diagnostic?"

"You'll find it in the functions catalogue. It enables the hospital system of your choice to monitor your health."

Conlan first patched through a visual link, which was easy, and gazed down at his leaking torso. Shortly he found the health monitoring function and studied its readout himself. It only confirmed what he already knew: he was dying. He allowed Krong access to that diagnosis.

"You're in a bad way, but I guess you don't need me to tell you that. I'm attaching a graphic for you now showing a future model of what we hope will shortly happen."

The attachment came through and Conlan hesitated before opening it. It could contain some military virus or something equally nasty, but he realised he was too tired to care. As he opened the attachment and viewed the scene displayed, and Moria's projections, he felt a steady vibration through the floor, growing in intensity.

"The positional drives have just started up," Krong noted.

"Can you see … outside? Can you see it?"

"Certainly can."

"Give me a visual link and I'll do what you want."

It came through quickly, and in his third eye Conlan gazed up through a chainglass dome across the Boh runcible, fusion flames of the positional drives gleaming in his vision. He rolled over and began crawling towards that vent, in the end not because he hated the Prador nor loved the Polity, but because of the sheer audacity of what that woman planned.

Hellish fire spewed across vacuum as the masers struck twelve targets out of a possible twenty, though it was difficult to be sure of the latter number since the missiles used many techniques of concealment. The ship's meteor defence laser struck five more, but the EM output of those close antimatter blasts threw his sensors into disarray. Two missiles struck his ship, the massive detonations hurling it back towards the runcible, a huge glowing dent in its hull.

Where are the rest?

His sensors finally unscrambled enough for him to see not one but three missiles now past his ship and bearing down on the runcible. A sudden detonation ensued and a drone tumbled out of the extremity of the explosion and then righted itself. A second detonation as a second missile passed through the enfilading fire from two other drones. Those drones were closer to the blast however, and their carrier signals flatlined. Despite the possibility of damage to the runcible, Immanence redirected masers to target the remaining missile—since there seemed few drones in the vicinity—but before his own weapons fired again the missile detonated, spreading a ball of white fire.

What?

He analysed what happened, and laughed his Pradorish laugh: the runcible's own meteor defences had fired up, destroying the missile. But the laughter did not last. For a moment he thought the runcible itself damaged from the close blast and now burning, then realised the flames he was seeing were too evenly spaced for that.

"Gnores, what is happening down there?"

"I am investigating now, Father. It seems that the engines used to position each section of the runcible are now operating."

Gnores did not sound particularly enthusiastic about his investigation, but Immanence could do nothing about that right then. He returned his attention to sensor data, seeing the Polity vessel decelerating hard and slightly altering its course, but that did not account for why it ceased firing. Immanence used manoeuvring thrusters to reposition his own ship to retain maximum cover of the runcible, then turned his attention to the damage received.

Numerous casualties and quite a lot of wreckage, but not sufficient to be concerned about. He redirected some of the stored power to memory metal layers in the hull and observed the dent gradually easing out. Again a scan of the runcible.

"Gnores, the runcible is spreading its five sections."

"Yes, I am aware of that... Father."

Immanence champed angrily. He again adjusted the position of his vessel, moving it further out to cover this expansion, still blocking line-of-sight from the Polity ship. But if Gnores did not come up with an explanation soon, Immanence decided he would move away. He did not like what was happening there. Then, at that moment, he became aware of a com channel signalling for his attention.

The Separatist.

"Explain," said Immanence succinctly.

"There's a Polity warship ... out there," said the one called Conlan.

"I am aware of that."

"They got through ... somehow. I'm injured."

"Explain!" Immanence spat.

"They want to destroy it."

Immanence spun round in frustration on his grav-motors.

"Explain yourself clearly, human!"

"The technicians—those few left here at Trajeen—they managed to break into the system—got control of the positional drives out there. They know you want it, and the Polity ship is there to destroy it. They're spreading it out... making it more difficult for you to cover."

"I see." Immanence cut the link. He eased his vessel out further, to keep the runcible covered. So this was why the Polity ship ceased firing: it was waiting until the five sections of the runcible presented easier targets and would then pick them off. Even now those sections lay on the edges of a circle a hundred kilometres across. The complex around it also separated, though Gnores and most of the second-children lay inside the largest piece attached to one gatepost.

"Gnores, recall all the second-children to the gatepost you presently occupy and concentrate your search there. Be thorough and be quick."

"Yeah...whatever."

Gnores would pay very heavily indeed for that. Immanence gazed through the cams on the first-child's carapace and saw that he was lingering by one of the corridors, peering down at a trail of human blood. Quickly reviewing the situation there, the captain saw that all the second-children were returning to that one gatepost, but was further angered to find that those inside that part of the complex were no longer searching for booby traps, but the injured human who had escaped. Gnashing his mandibles in frustration, Immanence cut the link and returned his attention to matters he could attend to now. Gnores would have to wait.

The Polity ship was manoeuvring again. Runcible a hundred and twenty kilometres wide. Immanence again shifted his ship to cover it; lower down towards Boh, the five gateposts marking points on the circumference of a perfect circle behind him. The Polity ship's tactics were admirable: Immanence needed to move his ship further and further out to cover the runcible, this meanwhile meant a greater chance of missiles getting round him. He would, he already decided, concentrate on defending the gatepost Gnores occupied, for snatching part of this runcible would be better than none at all.

Twenty seconds.

Moria was panicking, correction after correction, small stabs of the positional drives and adjustments to field strengths and energy feeds, calculations screaming through her mind like a hysterical crowd. The meniscus spread before her like a new horizon, wavering, seeming close to going out, the further gateposts out of sight. One small error and it would fail. Already the drain from the solar satellites had maxed out.

Fifteen seconds.

Fluctuation: G3. In her virtual vision the meniscus began bowing in between posts three and four. In less than a hundredth of a second an AI on the planet shut down the smaller runcible there for the evacuees, and opened its own processing space for her. The screaming crowd of calculations spilled in and spread, and gave her room for just one more. She ran it, sent the corrections, watched the bow straightening out again.

Ten seconds.

"You can do this?" Moria asked out loud.

Over the tumult she heard, "Desperate diseases have desperate remedies."

Yeah—right.

Five seconds.

It hurtled into view, tumbling end over end, two hundred kilometres across at its widest point, trillions of tonnes of asteroidal iron and stone: *Vina*—the fast moon. The last seconds counted down as slow as years as the moon loomed before her—a crushing, unimaginable force.

"Work, damn you!" Moria screamed.

The moon tumbled into the meniscus, gone. Moria released her hold and errors stacked a thousandfold. The runcible went out.

Instantly alerted, Immanence turned to his screens, and for a moment could not comprehend the shimmering circle appearing behind his ship, two hundred and forty kilometres across. In panic he started main engines, and manoeuvring thrusters to turn his ship, and began directing weapons towards this new threat. Missiles launched and all four particle cannons began firing.

"Scrabbler!" he bellowed. "Gnores!" And then, "Vagu—"

Something briefly occupied the circle and grew immense before him. Immanence did not even have the time to realise what it must be. Sensors transmitted brightness and went out as annihilation arrived.

Tomalon expected to see the moon hurtling out, but it came so much faster than that. Just a flicker between the runcible and the Prador ship, then an explosion that briefly blanked out sensors within the human visual range. They came back to reveal a streak of incandescence across space, a cometary tail of gaseous iron and rock, and glimmering tarry streaks of exotic metal, already hardening in vacuum into objects almost with the appearance of bones.

"*It worked,*" said Tomalon.

"*We were lucky,*" Occam replied. "*Now we need to be stronger, and better.*"

Jebel Krong felt something loosen inside his chest, but that was all—no fierce joy, no relief. Perhaps the drugs dulled his senses too much. Maybe he would feel it later.

Lindy let out a series of whoops and was now lying on her back staring up at the tail of fire stretching out from Boh. Urbanus showed no reaction at all, but now turned towards him.

"There are still Prador here on the runcible," the Golem reminded them.

"Yeah, but over on Gatepost One, not here. Let's at least celebrate that."

Urbanus shrugged.

Annoyed, Jebel decided to try another party.

"*Well, what did you think of that?*" he sent to Conlan.

"Oh Christ! Help me!"

"Give me visual," Jebel instructed.

"Ah fuck you!"

This last might well have been addressed to Jebel, but he rather thought the source of Conlan's rage and fear more imminent. But visual came through, nevertheless.

Mandibles loomed right in front of Conlan's face. The view changed abruptly, and now the man gazed down at a claw closed around his waist as he was thrust backwards. A subliminal glimpse then inside a small room: smashed computer console, some second-children skittering about excitedly, a bed up against one wall, torn in half. Had Conlan tried to hide underneath it?

"What's happening, Conlan?"

"Stuck me to the wall!"

The second-children were now doing something—hooking up bags and pipes. Jebel checked the man's health readout and realised that though he remained mortally wounded, the Prador were giving him fluids and stimulant drugs intravenously. They wanted to keep him alive for as long as possible. Jebel reached into his pocket and removed a small remote control, and still watching the scene through Conlan's eyes, he called up a particular designation on the remote's screen and held his thumb poised over the print and DNA reader pad.

"I can help you, Conlan, but only in one way."

"Aaargh!"

The big Prador in the room had torn away the temporary dressing around Conlan's torso, and now unravelled something Conlan only glimpsed before turning away, unable to bear the sight. Jebel lowered his thumb. Conlan's eyes opened on Prador mandibles munching something like bloody spaghetti, then the scene whited out and all contact fizzed away. The intense flash reached Jebel from over two hundred kilometres away. Hauling himself up a little he could just see that initial glare simmering down and now spreading into a glowing ball, slowly dispersing.

"Well that takes care of numerous problems," commented Urbanus.

"What was that?" asked Lindy.

"The mines on Gatepost One," Jebel replied.

"Conlan?"

"Yes," said Jebel Krong, his throat tight. He rubbed at the V-shaped scar on his cheek and realised his face was wet with tears. Utterly ridiculous that this last act—killing someone no better than the Prador themselves—finally elicited a response. But he saw if for what it was: a streak of fire through space was just too dispassionate, and this last had been up close, and personal.

Vagule hung in space utterly devoid of purpose as he observed the smear of gas and debris that was all that remained of his home. He eyed the fading light of the other explosion that killed the rest of his kin, and cold thoughts cycled in his cold mind.

"Father?" he queried over the ether.

"Kill the humans! Kill the Humans!" chanted the remaining second-child drones as they accelerated towards the approaching Polity dreadnought.

Vagule felt the sudden impulse to follow them. Wasn't this his purpose?

"They will not manage to kill any humans," Pogrom observed. "But their loyalty is admirable."

Vagule absorbed that: though to kill humans was his purpose as a war drone, that purpose remained implicit rather than a direct order from his father, therefore he found he could get around it, especially since the chances of fulfilling said purpose in these circumstances seemed remote. The only problem was that once round it he began to feel empty again.

"We must return home and report this," said Pogrom.

Vagule spied the other war drone drawing close, burns and scars on its armour from an explosion that destroyed other drones. Once again Vagule absorbed the underlying message. Reporting this incident was utterly proper, it was the returning home bit that seemed problematic: drones did not contain U-space drives.

"Do you agree?" asked Pogrom.

If they stayed here they would certainly end up being destroyed by the Polity dreadnought. If they headed for the planet, their chances of survival were just as limited, the greater likelihood being that the dreadnought would detect them long before they reached it.

"It seems reasonable," Vagule tentatively agreed.

"Let us make an inventory of our resources," Pogrom suggested.

With sufficient power they could survive for centuries, for in essence they were no longer organic creatures. They found both their power levels to be at a similar level, and began analysing astrogation data for the best route home. For both of them, the best option was for them to link up, and use one fusion burn of eight hours to throw them towards the nearest star, saving some fuel to manoeuvre when they got there. Upon their arrival they would probably be able to find useable ice to convert into fuel and sunlight on which to recharge power cells. During the intervening time, they held sufficient power to maintain their facsimile of life. Many such stopovers would be necessary. *Many*.

Vagule and Pogrom linked using extensible grabs, adjusted their attitude to the stars and fired up their drives. Behind them they observed fires flaring and going out as the second-child drones drew close enough to the Polity dreadnought for it to detect them, and erase them. Their defiant cries swiftly died. Eight hours later Vagule and Pogrom shut down their drives, and hurtled through dark to the first of eight hundred distant lights. They did finally arrive in what had once been the Prador Second Kingdom, and it was a strange and alien place. But they were stranger and more alien still after their fifty-three-century journey.

Exhausted, Moria detached her optic cable and let it drop. She gazed across at George, his forehead down on the table and utterly still. She wondered if this had killed him as she reached out to unplug his optic cable, but the moment it came free he jerked, placed the flat of his hand on the pseudo wood and slowly pushed himself upright.

"Are you all right?" she asked, wondering what proverb he would use for his reply.

He said nothing, just stared at her.

Moria closed her eyes for a moment. They had done it, she watched it all through the test sensors, but somehow this just did not seem to satisfy and she felt the need for a more human confirmation.

"Come on," she said, pulling at the shoulder of his uniform. She stood, her legs shaking and something hollow nestling under her breastbone. George stood also, though she had not expected him to. She led the way out into the corridor, for a moment unable to decide which way to go, unable to simply find her way in this complex even after all she had just achieved. Then she worked it out and headed off. George stumbled along behind her and she wondered if his operation of the internal runcible systems had burnt out what remained of his mind. There was blood leaking from behind his aug and his mouth hung open with a trickle of saliva shining on one side.

Finally they reached the place where she first encountered

Jebel Krong. The windows here gave her the view she required. She walked over to stand before vacuum and reached out her right hand to press it against cool chainglass.

The gas giant itself stood out visibly larger than surrounding stars, and extending from it coiled a short tail of brightness, fading now. As she watched it she felt George's hand close about her left hand. She turned to look at him. He closed his mouth, reached up and wiped it.

He smiled and told her:

"And hand in hand, on the edge of the sand,
They danced by the light of the moon,
The moon,
The moon,
They danced by the light of the moon."